Back From The Dead

Back From The Dead

Light Shines as the Noonday Sun

R. C. JETTE

RESOURCE *Publications* • Eugene, Oregon

BACK FROM THE DEAD
Light Shines as the Noonday Sun

Resource Publications
An Imprint of Wipf and Stock Publishers
199 W. 8th Ave., Suite 3
Eugene, OR 97401

www.wipfandstock.com

PAPERBACK ISBN: 978-1-7252-6334-5
HARDCOVER ISBN: 978-1-7252-6335-2
EBOOK ISBN: 978-1-7252-6336-9

Manufactured in the U.S.A.   01/27/20

This book is dedicated to my Lord Jesus Christ who makes all things possible by faith!

Also, to my husband (Paul) who has been a continued encouragement to me. My daughter (Dawn) who has freed me up to write.

I would also like to mention my son (PJ) and his daughter (Keira). My daughter (Christina) and her sons, (Andrew, Matthew, and Joshua) and her daughter (Sarah) who awaits the grand reunion day. I also want to thank Susanna and Mike.

My heartfelt thanks is given to Wipf and Stock Publishers for their continued publication of my books under their Resource Publications. I thank their staff who have constantly made this challenge more tolerable. Special thanks is given to Matthew Wimer, Daniel Lanning, George Callihan, Shannon Carter, and Savanah Landerholm to whom words cannot convey my gratitude.

SANCTUARY

Still as the soul at rest
The place of solitude:
Prayer beckons to come
Within the silent shroud.
Tranquility is yearned
From heartache that engulfs:
Escape implies repose
From grief that encircles.
Faith begins to quiver
Like sand beneath the waves;
Foundation does fragment
Amidst bitter sadness.
Hurled wildly like a raft
On a turbulent sea,
Tempest begins to calm
Reaching—sanctuary.

Contents

Prologue

"O God, I've lost everything." Mark Nottingham said as he stood in his office. His eyes turned towards the picture of his maternal grandfather, Michael Rochester, and said. "I'm so sorry, grandfather. You started this company when just out of college. Now, Rochester Company is no more." He then focused his attention on a picture on his desk. "Dad, you tripled it after you received it. Now, ten years after I inherit, it's bankrupt."

Tears filled his eyes. "I've lost everything you both worked for." He falls to his knees. "Lord, help me. How did this happen? What about my wife and son? Where will we live? I've lost the house. What can I do for work?" He looked up. "Lord, I've failed you, my grandfather, my father, Faith, and Thomas Mark."

He laid prostrate on the floor and just cried out to the Lord for direction. "Lord, I don't know what to do. Please give me direction to overcome this obstacle." He laid silent for what seemed hours. All of a sudden, he got up. "Thank you, Lord. I'll do it. This time, I'll make sure of those I put into positions. It was my fault for not checking what they were doing with investments. I knew the couple weren't Christians, but I didn't think they'd embezzle millions." He rubbed the back of his neck with his right hand. "They hid it through a bogus company, destroyed all the records, and there's no trail to find the money." He gave a heavy sigh. "Yes, your word says we shouldn't be unequally yoked together with unbelievers. I always thought that meant in dating and marriage. Now, I know it doesn't matter what it is. Christians are to yoke up with those of like-minded faith." He paused. "How many times do Christians find themselves undone because they've yoked up with unbelievers in various endeavors?"

He was interrupted by the sound of the elevator. Taking a deep breath, he composed himself. He'd called Faith earlier, told her everything, and asked that she and their son come to the office to sort out personal things and take the pictures. As soon as Thomas entered the office, he gazed into his father's eyes. "Mom said we have to move and sell all our belongings. That doesn't mean our card collection, right?"

"Son, I know you're only ten, but someday you'll understand what's happened." Mark took his son's right hand into his hands. "I will tell you I trusted the wrong people, who weren't Christians, to handle things. I should've been alert, but I wasn't." He paused. "Thomas, make sure whoever you trust is led of God." He rubbed the back of his neck with his right hand. "About the card collection, it must be sold. While in prayer, the Lord told me to sell the card collection and start a new company and name it Nottingham, LLC."

"But where will we live? Mom said we can't stay in our house."

Faith interrupted. "Mark, my uncle left me that two-bedroom cottage on twenty acres near the lake he used to fish at." She sighed. "It's not what we've been used to, but we own it. At least we'll have a home."

Mark gave his wife a hug. "Praise the Lord! That twenty acres is near a main highway. I'll build Nottingham, LLC. on that property." He rubbed the back of his neck with his right hand. "It'll be tough for a little while, but with God all things are possible."

Faith smiled. "We've had things quite easy." She bit her bottom lip. "I don't know how many times we've told people to trust the Lord and live by faith." She chuckled. "Well, God is saying it's time to live what we've preached."

"Amen!" As long as we allow the Lord to lead us, we'll conquer this thing." Tears filled his eyes. "God is so faithful." He paused. "He'll show us how to live sparingly, only buy what we need, and come out on the other side of this storm victoriously."

Chapter 1

Walking Dead Man

DOGS BARKED AND HOWLED to the bewilderment of the inquisitive woman. Motioning with both hands, she yelled. "What's all the squeaking and clanking noise about? It has the dogs down the street out of sorts. I've never heard such a penetrating noise. It's most baffling. I mean, I've not heard such screeching and clanking before."

Her husband, who stood at the end of the driveway holding a trash bag, just shrugged his shoulders. His focus was on the strange sight down the street. Up the slight incline, squeaked the wheels of an old shopping cart full of green trash bags, bulging with empty pop cans, and clanking against the sides.

Standing on the porch, the woman bombarded her husband with questions. "What's that supposed to be? Is it a shopping cart? Is anyone pushing it? I mean, is it a child? Can you see how it's moving?" She paused. "Robert, are you listening to me? What do you see? I can't make it out from here. I mean, I forgot my glasses in the house."

Without a response, Robert Montgomery put his trash on the sidewalk and watched the cart. All of a sudden, he saw an old man, bent at the waist, thin arms stretched out, and boney fingers clenching the cart's handle hiding behind the load. The man's head hung down, his eyes watched the ground, as he pushed with all his might to gain momentum.

As the man reached him, Mr. Montgomery smiled. "You have quite a load there." Expecting a reply, he didn't anticipate what he saw. Up from behind the man's right arm, his head popped up, without looking at the source of the voice, and quickly returned to its former position. Startled by what he saw, Robert gasped as if viewing one from the dead.

Beady blue eyes, set deep in their sockets, had looked up in horror. Stringy blond hair covered a mere skull, sunken cheeks emphasized his nose, and the skeleton body resembled one from Auschwitz. A piece of twine, tied in a knot, held up tattered blue jeans. Tucked into the jeans was a rag held on by one button, and the flapping sole of the right shoe was kept in place with precision movement.

Martha joined her husband as the man continued pushing his cart toward the next house, wheels squealing, trash bags clanking against the sides, and his right shoe in rhythm to gather his booty. While she stood there, Mr. Montgomery put his left forefinger against his lips. Once the man was a good distance away, he looked at his wife and sighed. "I thought he was an old man, but his gait and features reveal a man of forty or so." He scratched the back of his head with his left hand. "He reminded me of those pictures we see of people who were in concentration camps. It was like he was a walking dead man." His eyebrows scrunched together. "I have no idea why he would bother with this neighborhood. The houses are so far apart. Unless, he figures a wealthy neighborhood would give him more cans." He gestured with his left hand. "It was quite shocking to say the least. All I could do was pray and ask the Lord to help the man."

Martha's face screwed up. "How does one become such a pathetic creature?" She paused. "I mean, it's just so sad." She bit her bottom lip. "Lord, please help that dreadful soul. Something is drastically wrong."

"Amen!" He gave a heavy sigh, walked away from the curb, and Martha followed. "I really feel I'm to do something to help him. But I'll have to seek the Lord for direction." He scratched the back of head with his left hand. "I know we've only been here a short while, but I don't remember seeing him until today. I wonder who he is?" He grabbed a few more trash bags and handed one to his wife. "Well, I think we better get these out to the road."

Robert was waiting at the curb the next Thursday evening. "Lord, I do feel such a strange pull toward this man." He paused and listened. "I hear the cart." He stood silent and waited for the man to approach. As he approached, Mr. Montgomery smiled. "It's certainly a lovely day. God has blessed us with such a beautiful day. Don't you think?"

Again, two beady blue eyes peered up without looking at him and his head quickly went back down to its original position. Robert scratched the back of his head with his left hand, and stood watching him step with precision movement to keep the right sole from tripping while he pushed the cart to the next neighbor. "Lord, what can I do? I'm so drawn to this man. What do you want me to do?" He clasped his hands together, ran into the house, and grabbed his hat. "Martha, I'm determined to see where the man goes. I feel strongly that I must help him." He threw up his hands. "At present, I've no idea what I'm to do. But I know the Lord's impressing me to follow him. He wants me to help." He put on his hat. "I'll be back later. I'm going to follow him from a distance and see where he goes."

Following the man was quite easy, for he moved so slowly. Robert Montgomery kept his distance and watched as the man went behind this big company. He continued to follow and saw him use his right hand to open the gate of a small cottage set way back on the property. The man pushed the cart up to the front door, parked it, and went in the door. Immediately, lights came on in the cottage.

Early the next morning, Robert visited the company to see if anyone knew who the man was. He met with the person who has been running the company for the past three years or so. "I'm David Kregel. I'm sort of the boss at present."

"I'm Robert Montgomery."

"Have a seat. Are you looking for work? We're hiring at present."

Mr. Montgomery shook his head. "No, I really don't know how to say why I'm here." He gave a heavy sigh. "Well, let me just say it. Do you know who lives in the cottage set way back on this property?"

David's eyebrows scrunched together. "That cottage has been empty for some time." He gestured with his right hand. "Why do you ask?"

"Well, for the past two weeks, there's this man who shows up on Thursday nights to go through people's trash to get empty pop cans." He scratched the back of his head with his left hand. "I followed him here, and he went into that cottage."

David jumped up. "Did you say you saw the man go into the cottage? How did he get in? You're sure he went in?"

Mr. Montgomery's eyebrows scrunched up. "He did something at the gate with his right hand, opened it, pushed the cart up to the front door, and went in. After he entered, the lights came on inside."

David grabbed his face with both hands. "Can you tell me what he looks like?"

"He's tall, extremely skinny, blue eyes, and light hair." He gestures with his left hand. "He's like a walking dead man. It was quite shocking to see."

David gave a quizzical look. "You said extremely skinny?"

"Yes. As a matter of fact, he reminds me of someone from a concentration camp. It's really quite alarming."

David stared at the picture hanging on the right side of his desk. "Would you say the man looked like him?"

"Well, I'll be. That looks exactly like him, except that man's quite built. The man I saw is nothing but skin and bones." He looked at David. "Who is that man?"

"His name is Tom." He sighed. "Okay, I'd really like to get my brother here, he was Tom's best friend until things changed. However, he and his family are visiting his wife's parents in Maine." He rubbed his temple with the fingers of his right hand. "I'll call him and bring him up-to-date. However, in the meantime, I think we better talk to Dr. Steinberg and get his advice on how to proceed. He should be in his office about two this afternoon. He's the company's counselor, but he helps counsel couples at church." He paused. "Anyway, can you be back here at two and meet with him?"

"I'll be here. I'm quite anxious to help this man." His eyebrows scrunched together. "What does that man in the picture have to do with the man I saw?"

"Believe me, Dr. Steinberg will make things clear. However, I need to check on something before you meet with the doctor." He rubbed his temple with the fingers of his right hand. "I really can't say more until I clarify things. If things go as I think, Dr. Steinberg will be able to help when you meet with him."

Chapter 2

The Good Samaritan

DAVID SET UP AN appointment for Robert Montgomery with Dr. Joseph Steinberg, the company counselor. Dr. Steinberg shook Robert's hand and gestured to a chair near his desk. "Would you have a seat?"

"Yes, thank you."

Dr. Steinberg sat back, pulled on his right earlobe, and said. "Would you please tell me all you told David?"

Robert nodded his head and proceeded to tell what he'd told David.

Once he finished, Dr. Steinberg questioned him. "Why are you here? What made you follow the man to the cottage?"

"I believe the Lord wants me to be the Good Samaritan and help him. When I prayed, I was given the parable of the Good Samaritan." He scratched the back of his head with his left hand. "It's almost overwhelming the impression from the Lord to help this man."

The doctor clasped his hands. "Praise the Lord!" He sat back in his chair. "The man you followed is Thomas Nottingham."

"That's the name of this company?"

"Yes, he's the owner."

Robert's eyebrows scrunched up. "What are you talking about? That man is picking up cans to survive. How can he own such a company and be in that condition?"

"It's a sad story." He paused. "But before I go on, would you like an iced tea?"

"Yes, as a matter of fact, I'd really like that."

He stood up, went over to the small refrigerator in the corner of his office, pulled out two bottles of iced tea, handed one to Robert, and sat back down.

"Thank you." He chuckled. "You sure can get thirsty down here."

The doctor took a drink of his tea and continued. "He inherited this company from his father, shortly before he turned thirty-four years of age. However, around his birthday, the business became a little unstable. Tom became possessed with running things, and he spent the next six months in his office or on business trips. We didn't think too much about it, because we all knew his father had lost the company he'd inherited when Tom was a young boy. Although he didn't go home much, he called his wife and children nightly. Abigail, his wife was so supportive. She knew what his family had to endure after his father lost the original business. Anyway, it seemed like the business was starting to become stable, and he began to go home on the weekends. However, things turned into a nightmare shortly after his thirty-fifth birthday when he became overwhelmed with grief."

"What happened?"

"His wife, Abigail and his two children, Samuel and Rachel were killed in an auto accident. Thomas was away on a business trip when it happened. Unable to cope with the heartache and self-condemnation, he cried for weeks and weeks. "I'm to blame. I should've been home. If I was home, she wouldn't have been driving. Oh, God, why didn't I send one of the managers? I neglected my family, who should have been my priority. Instead, I allowed the business to consume my time and thoughts."

"Oh my! How sad." He paused. "Has anyone tried to help him?"

"Of course, but we couldn't seem to break through the barrier of grief." He gestured with his right hand. "To put it in simple terms, Tom was in a severe state of depression. I could give a more clinical explanation, but I don't think it would be of much use to you."

"Why don't you try? I've had a lot of practice teaching, besides, I had psychology in college. I really didn't know if the Lord wanted me to be a pastor. If so, I'd have to know how to counsel a congregation." He took a sip of his iced tea. "However, after I graduated, the Lord made it clear he wanted me to teach at the Bible College."

The doctor nodded his head. "Okay." As you know, Tom was away on business, when the accident took place. After he heard the horrendous news, he flew right home and seemed all right until the funeral. That's when he lost it and kept crying what I told you earlier" He sighed. "From that point on, he started a downward cycle. He was enslaved in hopelessness and guilt. Pastor Jonathan Kregel and he were so close until the accident. Then something changed. He missed church often, and then stopped going all together." He took a drink of his iced tea. "We all hoped he would center his emotions on the business after the funeral. Instead, he ceased all activity, until there was a cessation of all effort."

Robert Montgomery rubbed his chin with his left hand. "I think I understand. In other words, Tom, enduring more than his emotional stamina was want, began a life of obscurity as protection against attachments. He gave into hopelessness and despair. This created a barrier freeing his heart from all emotions." He paused. "Am I correct so far?"

"That's very well stated. I couldn't have said it better myself."

"Wait a minute! Did you say his pastor is Jonathan Kregel?"

"Yes. He pastors Hope Tabernacle."

Mr. Montgomery threw up his hands. "No wonder, David Kregel looked so familiar to me."

Dr. Steinberg chuckled. "They're identical twins, except David still has all his hair, whereas, Jonathan is bald." He paused. "Do you go to Hope Tabernacle?"

"We moved down here a little over a month ago to be near my wife's sister who lost her husband. We've been going there a few weeks." He scratched the back of his head with his left hand. "It's like Tom Nottingham has left the world of the living."

"Exactly! As protection against the pain, he's closed himself in obscurity, apart from reality. That's the irony of it all, because it's the opposite of his personality. Tom wasn't a loner and was noted for his compassion toward anyone isolated. If a worker or someone from the church appeared lonely, he would have them over his house for supper, a barbecue, or whatever."

"But why isn't he here? What's he doing in that cottage? Hasn't anyone checked up on him?" He paused. "I'm not trying to judge, but you all seem to be Christians. Jesus said people will know we're his disciples by our love toward one another. Why is the man alone and in such a dreadful state? Why haven't any of you tried to help him?" He gave a heavy sigh. "I mean, did he get on alcohol or drugs? How did he get into such a state?"

"Let me explain. We all love him and did all we could." He pulled his earlobe with his right thumb and forefinger. "No, he never drank or did drugs. Outside of grief and self-condemnation, we couldn't find any dependencies."

"Then what happened?"

"Right after the funeral, he gave the grounds keeper his house, and moved into the keeper's cottage. Then he had the lawn pulled up, had cement poured around it, and had that twelve-foot fence put up. Apparently, the gate only opens with his right hand." He took a drink of his iced tea. "At first, we just thought he wanted to be left alone." He paused. "We gave him space, so he could heal of his grief. However, he was barely in his office, just stayed locked up in the cottage." He sat back and folded his arms. "At first, when we'd ask him to lunch, he'd respond, 'Not today.' After a couple of months, he'd answer, 'Just leave me alone.' In the end, he just stared like a mute, deaf, and dumb. He wouldn't look any of us in the eyes. Although we knew this wasn't Tom, we couldn't break through his self-made wall. We figured it would be a matter of time, and he'd come around." He threw up his hands. " Then one day, he came in and told David he was leaving on vacation and to handle things until he came back." He leaned forward. "We were all elated that he was taking a vacation and felt confident that would bring about his healing." He sighed. "However, that was about three years ago." He sat back. "We've not heard a word from him and couldn't track him down. We had no idea if he was dead or alive, until you came in this morning." He took a drink of his iced tea. "David wanted to check and make sure it was him, so he went to the gate and called out to him. Tom looked out the window and immediately shut the shade."

"So, it's him?"

"Oh yes, David has no doubt."

"But isn't his being back a positive sign? I mean, he could be starting an upward cycle out of his depression. If he's back, the Lord must be working in his life." He took a drink of his iced tea. "I feel strongly that God wants to use me in his recovery. He gave me the Good Samaritan. I'll admit I'm at a loss at what to do, but I believe the Lord is leading me in this thing." He scratched the back of his head with his left hand. "I had thought of going to the cottage, but the Lord strongly impressed me to stay away from his safe haven. At present, it seems to be his refuge. If he's bothered, he may leave again." He paused. "It's like the Lord is using the cottage as a sanctuary drawing Tom into a place of solitude where he can calm the tempest of heartache that has Tom engulfed. I just know the Lord has impressed me Tom needs to be restored, and he must be in that cottage for it to happen."

"Yes, yes. I agree. I'll make sure none go near it." He paused. "I know David did, but it was to make sure it was Tom. However, he'll not go near it again. Unless Tom contacts us, we'll leave him alone and allow God to do what He's doing." He took a drink of his iced tea. "We'll not stand in your way. I believe you're right that something is beginning to happen. I had thought to put him in the hospital before he left. But when I prayed, the Lord strongly impressed me to do nothing but pray for him. God didn't want us interfering, or we could do more damage. He was going to do a work in Tom and any interference could hinder the healing that needed to take place. So, I just committed him into the Lord's hands."

"That's what I did the first time I saw him, but the Lord gave me the parable of the Good Samaritan." He scratched the back of his head with his left hand. "That made it quite obvious I'm to do more than pray."

Dr. Steinberg clasped his hands. "I must admit I'm overjoyed he's back. There were times, I couldn't sleep praying for him. I've known him from almost the beginning of his father starting this company. Tom was about fifteen when I met him. That's over twenty years ago." He paused. "He reminds me of my favorite nephew, so I really took to him. I truly believe it was the Lord impressing me he was in a bad way and needed prayer." He sighed. "At present, I'm concerned about his eating. You said he looks like someone from a concentration camp. David's brief sight of him confirmed your description." He pulled his right earlobe with his right thumb and forefinger. "That's troubling me. However, God has been taking care of him this long. I must get out of my emotions and trust him to continue." He paused. "I wonder if I could wait until the lights are off in the cottage and put groceries outside the gate in a covered bin?" He threw his head against the back of his chair. "There I go again trying to take matters into my own hands. It's a good thing Pastor Kregel isn't here. He'd be reprimanding me for a lack of faith."

Mr. Montgomery stood up. "Believe me, I've been wondering how to feed him. But as you said, we have to trust God. He's brought him back, and now we must be led by his Holy Spirit to do what's right." He paused. "Well, I need to get home and seek the Lord for direction."

The doctor reached out to shake Robert's hand. "I'll pray for the Lord's guidance."

"Amen! I'm at a loss about what to do at present, but God knows how to handle this situation." He paused. "I keep hearing to trust in the Lord with all my heart and lean not unto my own understanding." He chuckled. "It's clear what's going to be done will be beyond my comprehension."

Chapter 3

A Cocoon of Grief

ROBERT MONTGOMERY KNEW ONLY prayer and fasting would help him gain wisdom in this situation. He realized Thomas Nottingham was a man cocooned in severe grief. In order for him to be restored, Robert had to be led of God. "Lord, I truly wish Pastor Kregel was back in town. He was his best friend, and he would know more about him than anyone else that I've talked to." He sighed. "Well, he's visiting his wife's family in Maine." He chuckled. "Yes Lord, I know you know him better than anyone. Please take care of his mental and physical well-being and reveal to me how to help break through his barrier of grief."

Martha Montgomery heard him pray. "Robert, is there anything I can do to help? I'm so saddened about what you told me about this man. I mean, he's been through so much." She paused. "If he's really a Christian, he'll come through once he stops looking at his turbulent sea of grief and looks to the Lord." She bit her bottom lip. "How to help him to focus on the Lord and not his loss is the question." She put her hands on her hips. "I'm sure God will lead you in what to do. I mean, he's always faithful."

"I just know the Lord has placed him on my heart and told me to be the Good Samaritan that helps him."

"How can you be that? I mean, he's not lying on the side of the road beaten by thieves. You don't have a donkey. How can you pour oil and wine in his wounds? You can't take him to the Inn to rest."

He took her face between both hands. "Martha, I know you've only been a Christian for about six months." He kissed her forehead. "However, this all has a spiritual significance. When God told me to be the Good Samaritan, he meant for me to help heal his wounds through prayer and fasting, the word of God, the love of God, and allow the Holy Spirit to break through his wall of grief and bring about healing."

Martha bit her bottom lip. "I do have so much to learn, and I'm thankful for your patience. I know you became born again on our honeymoon, and you prayed for almost forty years for me to see truth." She paused. "But is there any way to learn faster? I mean, is there a course or something that can be taken? You taught at the Bible College before retiring. I mean, is there a way to grow faster?"

"We grow through reading our Bible, asking the Holy Spirit to interpret the Scriptures to us, and then living the revelations the Spirit gives us. There are no quick courses in the natural to help us grow spiritually." He rubbed his chin with his left hand. "You continue to be faithful in prayer, reading his word, and being led by the Holy Spirit." He paused. "Have you finished reading your Sunday school lesson for tomorrow?"

She threw up her hands. "Oh dear, I've been so preoccupied with this Thomas Nottingham thing that I forgot to finish it. I need to learn to put first things first. I mean, how will I grow if I don't keep focused on the spiritual things and not on the physical." She paused. "Pastor Kregel preached about that last Sunday. He said too many Christians remain babies because they don't focus on spiritual growth and stay too focused on this world and its so-called pleasures." She put her hands on her hips. "That's it, I'm going to finish it right now. Then I'll pray for you to get direction from the Lord to help Tom."

"Thank you, I could use the prayer." He paused. "You do need to learn to calm down and rest in the Lord. Being anxious about things will only keep your mind on what you aren't doing instead of seeing you're growing. Remember, a baby doesn't get up and walk the day its born. It doesn't feed itself the day its born. It doesn't dress itself the day its born. As you can see it takes time for a physical baby to mature, you must see it takes time for a spiritual baby to mature. You take one baby step at a time and before you know it, you'll be running. In other words, you'll be off the milk and onto the strong meat of the mature Christian."

When they entered Hope Tabernacle on Sunday morning, Pastor Jonathan Kregel was waiting. He quickly went over to Robert and asked if he would step into his office. Robert turned to Martha. "You go to Sunday school, and I'll see you in the sanctuary after." He scratched the back of his head with his left hand. "I think it's imperative for me to speak with the pastor."

Martha nodded her head. "Yes, it's more needful for me to be learning. I mean, I've determined to make the Lord's will my top priority. I think he's given me a schedule to help me grow in knowledge, wisdom, and understanding of his word." She paused. "I believe he wants me to listen to all your lectures given about the Bible. I mean, I know you suggested it, but I now see it will be an incredible help."

As she walked away, Robert followed the pastor to his office. "I'm really surprised to see you. Your brother told me you and your family were in Maine." He smiled. "I must admit I prayed I would get to talk to you about Thomas Nottingham."

The pastor opened his office door and had Robert go in ahead. Once inside, he locked the door and closed the blind. "I don't want any interruptions. We don't have much time before service, and I felt compelled to talk to you." He rubbed the top of his bald head with his right hand. "As soon as David called me, I made plans for us to return as quickly as possible. We just got in at 1:30 this morning." He bit the hangnail on his right hand. "Anyway, on the way home, I called Dr. Steinberg who told me all you talked about. He said the Lord impressed you to be the Good Samaritan that is instrumental in Tom's healing." Tears filled his eyes. "It bore witness with my spirit, and that's why I knew I must see you immediately." Would you like a coffee? I think I really need one."

"No, thank you." He gestured with his left hand. "You go right ahead. I limit myself to one cup of coffee a day. It seems to give me the jitters if I drink more. I find I tolerate tea better."

Pastor Kregel poured himself a coffee and sat back in his chair. "My heart's so heavy and happy at the same time about Tom coming back. He was best man at our wedding, and I was best man at his wedding. You see, we were in school together, went to Bible College together, and were like brothers. David and I may be twins, but he loved sports, and I didn't. We both had such different hobbies. His was all sports and mine was drawing and painting." He paused. "You see that painting hanging behind my desk, Tom did it. He's a better artist than me."

"Wow!" He's talented. What a beautiful scenery." He paused. "Is he the one who wrote the Scripture that with God nothing is impossible?"

"Yes, if he hadn't been involved in his father's business, he truly wanted to be a preacher. That's why he got a degree in theology." He rubbed his bald head with his right hand. "Now, let's see how to begin this. I'm full of questions. The Lord keeps telling me not to be anxious, pray, and thank him that Tom is back." He sipped his coffee. "Do you have any idea concerning what God wants you to do?"

"Yes, he's led me into prayer and fasting for several days. He wants me to use his word, extend the love of Christ, and allow the Holy Spirit to pour the wine and oil of healing into him."

"Praise the Lord! I haven't ceased to pray for him since the accident." His eyes teared. "I told the Lord I don't know how I would've reacted if I lost my whole family. I just prayed that his grace would get Tom through, but I didn't expect to be still praying about four years later." He leaned forward. "It's rather strange, but you resemble Tom's father. Mark had gray hair, hazel eyes, and was about your size. It's uncanny how much you bear a resemblance to him." His eyebrows scrunched together. "I wonder if that's why God is going to use you?" He gestured with both hands. "Anyway, I think it all stems from something Tom's father told him after he lost the company his maternal grandfather started. You see, his mother inherited the cottage and the land the company is on from an uncle. But his father told him that he lost the company, their house, and all assets because he trusted the wrong people to handle things in the business. Apparently, they embezzled millions of dollars that couldn't be traced." He sipped his coffee. "His father told him to always check everything. Tom never really paid much attention to that advice until after he inherited the company, and there was instability in it. His fear of losing the business started him to be so conscious of what everyone was doing. He started to work late into the night and weekends for about six months. Although things seemed to be improving, Tom was relentless in watching what everyone was doing." He sipped his coffee. "I believe the fear of ending up like he and his family living in the cottage for five years until his father had Nottingham, LLC making a profit consumed him. He had several others who could have taken the trips. But by this time, he couldn't let go and let others." He looked at his watch. "Anyway, while he was on a business trip, the accident occurred. Abigail, his wife, was driving back from a church cookout, when this drunk driver drove into them. He was going so fast that he rammed them against the barrier. They were all killed instantly."

Mr. Montgomery hung his head. "All of this is so sad. But we have to believe that something good will come from this. I know it's hard to see it now, but God's word doesn't lie."

"Amen! I keep hearing that every time I pray for Tom." He took sip of his coffee. "All I know is that he seemed to be oblivious to anyone around him. He lost all interest in his business dealings." He paused. "As a matter of fact, he turned it all over to David who had no control of any of it before that day. Praise God, though, David was God's choice. He's not only stabilized it, but has tripled its business. It's really thriving."

"That's good to hear." He paused. "At present, if Tom is to come back from the dead, so to speak, only God knows how to break down the barrier. He's woven in a cocoon of self-protection that only God can breach." He scratched the back of his head with his left hand. "Where's Tom's family? I've not heard any mention of a family."

"Apparently, his mother was an only child as were her parents. His father, as far as I know, has a distant cousin named Grace who is now widowed. Her daughter Hannah is a little younger than Tom.

She's widowed with four-year-old twins. However, neither one has ever met Tom. They live way up in Montana." He bit the hangnail on his right thumb. "This may be off the subject, but I feel strongly the Lord wants me to tell you about Hannah. She married the music minister in their church about five years ago. Anyway, a month after they returned from their six-week honeymoon, his boyfriend murdered Ronald."

Robert shook his head and blinked his eyes. "Did I hear you say his boyfriend?"

"Yes, apparently he was gay and didn't want his family or the church to find out. So he married Hannah as a cover-up. She was devastated to find that she had been so beguiled. How could she not see signs. Her greatest battle was that she didn't really pray about it. She knew his parents. He played the piano, sang beautifully, and always seemed to be a godly man." He leaned forward. "However, a couple of months after Ronald's death, she discovered she was about three months pregnant. With all the ordeal of everyone discovering he was gay, she assumed that's why she wasn't feeling too well."

"Oh my! That's quite sad." He gestured with his hands. "I don't mean about her pregnancy, but the gay husband." He scratched the back of his head with his left hand. "My question is he how did he sit under Holy Ghost preaching and not be convicted. Didn't he read his Bible? After all, Romans chapter 1 makes clear that those who changed the truth of God into a lie and worshipped and served the creature more than the Creator were given over unto vile or despicable affections. Even the women changed the natural use into that which is against nature. Also the men, leaving the natural use of the woman, burned in their lust one toward another; men with men. So, because they didn't want to retain God in their knowledge, God gave them over to a reprobate or degenerate mind." He paused. "Perhaps, he was given over to the reprobate mind, because he'd already had his conscience seared with a hot iron through his perverted desire."

"I know what you mean." He bit the hangnail on his right hand. "I've talked to Grace and Hannah and they have both struggled as to how they could've been so beguiled by the man." He took a sip of his coffee. " Anyway, it was Tom's parents who helped Grace and

Hannah after Grace's husband died. Plus, they put Hannah through college. She has a degree in Business Administration. But after she had the twins, she had to quit her job. She wouldn't put them in a daycare." He rubbed his bald head with his right hand. "I haven't heard from them for some time. I told Grace I'd call when Tom came back."

"Hannah sounds like a devoted Christian who got messed up with a white-walled sepulcher or a wolf in sheep's clothing. Even the most committed Christian, if not careful, can be beguiled by the snakes hidden in the church."

Pastor Kregel stood up and put his hand on Robert's right shoulder. "Lord, I thank you for this man of God you've chosen to help Tom. I ask you to give him an anointing that will break the yolk and shatter the chains that have Tom imprisoned in this grief and self-condemnation. We bind the powers of Hell that should try to hinder the miracle you are about to perform and believe you for complete healing. In the mighty Name of Jesus!"

"Amen!" Robert Montgomery grabbed the pastor's hand with both hands. "I feel such an incredible victory is about to take place. At the same time, the Lord impressed me not to quit. I believe a battle is ahead, but I know Christ has conquered the powers of Hell. All I have to do is stand in his armor and fight with Tom through to the conquest."

Pastor Kregel gave Robert a hug. "I can't get over how much you remind me of Tom's father. He was an incredible man of faith. He told me that when you find yourself in a place that the only thing you can do is trust God, it does something to your faith walk. He would be sixty-seven. However, he died of a heart attack at sixty-two." He paused. If you don't mind my asking. What's your age?"

"I'm sixty-three."

The pastor looked at his watch. "I have to get to the sanctuary. I'm not preaching this morning, Pastor Micah, the youth pastor is." He gestured with both hands. "I'm not supposed to be here today." He stopped, rubbed his bald head with his right hand, and gazed at Robert. "We go to the Family Buffet on Sunday after church. It's much easier on Tabitha with how hectic Sunday's can be. Especially now that she's expecting our third child, a girl. We have twin boys,

Amos and Joel, who are almost thirteen." He bit the hangnail on his right thumb. "Anyway, if you and your wife aren't busy after service, could you join us for lunch? The boys are going with David to play basketball at his house and have a barbecue."

Robert scratched the back of head with his left hand. "I've been in prayer and fasting since Thursday night, but I sense I'm to go." He smiled. "I do believe Martha and I would be pleased to join you and your wife for lunch." He paused. "We never had children. I was busy teaching at Fountain Bible College, and Martha's a registered nurse. It's like we were so busy that we didn't realize we were childless until I retired at sixty-two." He paused. "Martha didn't get saved until several months ago. Perhaps that's why. Or it's because God has other plans."

"God knows what he's doing." He headed towards his office door. "Well, let's get to the sanctuary, and we'll get together for lunch."

The Family Buffet was rather crowded, but the owner, Mr. Smith, had the pastor's usual table reserved. Pastor Kregel introduced Robert and Martha Montgomery to him, as they were heading to the table. After they all sat down. Robert looked around. "This place must serve some good food, or it's the only place around."

Tabitha leaned forward. "It's about the only place around that's not a fast food, but Mrs. Smith is an incredible cook." She gestured with both hands. "She makes everything taste like you're eating in your mother's kitchen." She gestured towards the buffet area. "Those are their two sons who keep everything full, and their wives help Mrs. Smith with the cooking."

Martha bit her bottom lip. "That's what I call a family affair." She paused. "If we'd been blessed with children, I would've liked us to be like that." She hung her head. "However, Robert had enough trouble trying to get me to see that God was a loving heavenly Father. I stopped going to church when I was thirteen. I mean, after my dad left with the secretary of the church, I wanted nothing to do with a God who would allow him to do such a thing to my mother, my sister, and me." She paused. "Sorry, I know I tend to rattle on so. However, I must add that my mother and sister never gave up on God. I mean, my mother said it wasn't God, but my father who chose to rebel against God's word. She said people have a free will to choose what they do or don't do." She gestured with her right hand. "I didn't really understand that until one of my patients told me what happened to her as a child and how she thanked God for helping her through it. I asked how she could thank God, when he could have stopped what was done." She took a drink of water. "Margaret, that was her name, looked me in the eyes and asked me a question. She asked if I'd ever done something that hurt someone else. I told her about the time I was angry at my sister for not letting me wear her dress to a cookout, because she was going to wear it. Anyway, I'd called her a horrible name, and she cried for days. Well, she then asked why God didn't stop me. I looked dumbfounded. Margaret then laughed and said he couldn't stop me because I was angry and wanted satisfaction by hurting my sister. She said that was my free-will. God will not stop me from doing what I choose to do." Tears filled her eyes. "I mean, it was like scales fell from my eyes, and I finally saw what my mother, my sister, and my husband had been trying to tell me for years. I couldn't tell my mother, because she'd been dead for twenty years. However, I immediately called Robert, and after that I called my sister and told her. That's when I found out her husband had died that morning. She was trying to pull herself together to call." She gave out a heavy sigh. "Robert was retired, and I knew I could get a job at any hospital if I wanted to, so we moved down here to be close to Mary." She paused. "Her name is Mary Simpson. She was sick today and that's why she wasn't in church."

The pastor nodded his head. "Yes. I know who she is. Her husband, Pete used to teach adult Sunday school. That's why we have different teachers at present. The Lord hasn't revealed to me who to appoint."

Robert rubbed his chin with his left hand. "I do believe we should get our food and talk some more after." He chuckled. "It's quite obvious the Lord has released me from the fasting. All those aromas are making my stomach growl."

Martha blushed. "I'm so sorry. I mean, I really need to stop rattling on."

Tabitha reached over and touched her right hand. "For some reason, my mother was the same way. Whatever was in her heart, she just blurted it out. She had me when she was forty-five. I'm now into the fifth month of my second pregnancy at thirty-six. Anyway, she died ten years ago at the age of seventy-three." She gave a tender smile. "What I'm trying to say is I understand."

Pastor Kregel stood up. "Well, I'm quite hungry. If you'll all follow me, let's get our food."

Robert was the first to compliment the meal. "This is simply delicious. Perhaps, I'm eating more than normal, but it's so good." He chuckled. "I didn't realize I could eat this much food after fasting. It's definitely the Lord."

Pastor Kregel laughed. "I know what you mean. Before we left for Maine, I broke a fast on chicken soup, and I was full."

Martha sighed. "I can cook, but it doesn't taste like this. I mean, I think we've found where we'll be eating when we go out to eat." She gazed at her husband. "I don't think we've ever had food this scrumptious." She bit her bottom lip. "My mother was a good cook, and everyone bragged about it. But she never cooked like this. I mean, this is the tastiest food I've ever had."

Tabitha sat back and folded her arms. "I told you Mrs. Smith's makes you feel like you're eating in your mother's kitchen."

Robert scratched the back of his head with his left hand. "I've never had any complaints about Martha's cooking, but I must admit this is exceptional."

Pastor Kregel sat back, and his eyes filled with tears. "Tom, Abigail, Rachel, and Samuel used to join us for Sunday lunch before everything happened. I miss them so much." He touched Robert's right hand. "My heart was excited when David called me about you. Now that I've met you, its full of expectation. I really believe God is about to move in Tom's life." He rubbed his bald head with his right hand. "I sense the Lord doesn't want any of us interfering. We're to be in prayer and be there if you need us for anything. Otherwise, it's you he's chosen to be his Good Samaritan."

"I don't know what he wants me to do, but I'll pray through. He has a plan, and I will be led of him." He rubbed his chin with his left thumb and forefinger. "There is an incredible thing happening in my heart concerning that young man. God used the Good Samaritan to bring healing to the man that fell among thieves, and I believe that he's about do so to Tom Nottingham."

Chapter 4

Adoptive Parents

Jonathan heard that Hannah's mother had passed away when David dropped the twins off Sunday night. Apparently, a college buddy of David's, lives in the same town, and called David earlier. He'd been out of town for several weeks, and just found out.

Jonathan was surprised Hannah hadn't called the church to tell him. First thing Monday morning, he called to see how she was doing. "Hannah, this is Pastor Jonathan Kregel. I know this is a different number, but I'm calling from home and not my office. I'm so sorry to hear about your mother." He paused. "I just found out about it late last night."

Hannah cleared her throat. "Thank you, pastor. My mother mentioned you often. She kept praying for Tom, and believed God would bring him back. There were times she wished she had known him, but it was Mark and Faith who visited when Tom was away at Bible Camp every summer. Then when Tom was in college, he spent his summer vacation on a mission trip." She paused. "After that, he was married. Anyway, he never came with them to Montana."

"What are you going to do now? How are you and the twins?"

She sighed into the phone. "To be honest, I'd leave this cold climate. I was seriously thinking of moving down there, but don't know how to see about a house. After the murder of Ronald, I moved in with my mother. When the twins were born, you know I quit my job. We couldn't afford the house. So, my mother sold it, and we moved into a two-bedroom apartment. I worked third shift at the local Marty's Supercenter. I'd have breakfast with Mom and the twins, play with them for a while, and Mom watched them so I could sleep until supper." She started to cry. "I don't know what to do. I've been praying for direction. Mom left me an insurance policy of $25,000. However, it cost over ten for her funeral. I've no family to watch the twins while I work." She cleared her throat. "I'm sorry for unloading on you. As a pastor, a husband, and father, you have enough on your plate." She paused. "Anyway, thank you for your call. I really appreciate it."

Jonathan stood up from his chair. "Listen, I'm hearing something from the Lord. Let me look into it, and I'll get back with you. Just don't make any moves until you hear from me. I believe God is already moving in this thing."

"Really! Praise God!" She giggled. "God told me to call you, but I couldn't find Mom's phone book." She paused. "I couldn't remember your last name or the name of your church. When you called and said who you were, I remembered it was Kregel. Anyway, I won't do a thing until I hear from you."

Jonathan hung up the phone and sat down in his recliner. "Lord, how do I mention this to him? It does seem to be a bit much to ask a complete stranger, but I know it's you directing."

Robert was taking his morning swim when Pastor Kregel arrived at the Montgomery's. Martha was listening to Robert's lectures when the doorbell rang. As she opened the door, her jaw dropped. "Pastor Kregel, what are you doing here? I mean, not that you're not welcome. It's just I didn't expect to open the door and find you standing here. Is something wrong? I mean, are you okay? Do you have news about Thomas Nottingham?" She bit her bottom lip. "I'm sorry. I haven't given you chance to say anything." She stepped away from door. "Please come in. Robert's taking his morning swim. You're welcome to come out to the pool, or do you want me to go get him?"

"No, let him have his swim. I'll just follow you out there." He looked around in amazement. "I had no idea this was such a huge house. It's so grand looking." He grabbed his head with both hands. "This is really quite astonishing. I knew the houses in this neighborhood are called Mansions, but I've only been in the Taylor's. It's half this size and I thought it was huge. It was nothing like this." He gestured with his right hand. "I don't believe I've ever seen such luxurious furnishings." He paused. "You two must be quite comfortably setup." His face flushed. "I'm sorry for that. What you are is none of my business. It's just that I was astonished when I came in."

At that, Robert was coming in from the pool and chuckled. "Yes, my father owned a chain of hardware stores. He sold everything before he died, because he knew I'd not be able to take over. I loved what I was doing, and he didn't want me to leave my job. Both my parents became saved after I did." He scratched the back of his head with his left hand. "Anyway, I really didn't have to work if I didn't want to. I'm rather a wealthy man." His eyebrows scrunched together. "If you don't mind me asking, what are you doing here? Is there news about Tom?"

The pastor rubbed his bald head with his right hand. "It's not about Tom. It's about his distant cousin I told you about. Well, Grace has passed away, and Hannah and the twins are in need of help."

Robert's eyebrows scrunched together. "What do you mean?"

"I told you Hannah wouldn't leave the twins in a daycare. Anyway, she was working third shift to support them all. It's a long story, but I believe the Lord wanted me to ask you to take them in." He put up his right hand. "I know it's a lot to ask, and I wouldn't have done such a thing if I didn't feel this strong impression from the Lord to do so." He gestured with both hands. "Of course, I had no idea you lived in such affluence. I only asked because the Lord wanted me to."

Robert walked away and left the pastor and Martha standing there looking at each other. When he returned, he had this old picture of a young woman and two small children. "That was my great-great-grandmother. Lately, the Lord has constantly placed this picture in my mind. I asked what it meant, but I just kept getting the picture. Now, I know the Lord was showing me it because of Hannah and the twins." He paused. "What are the twins, boys, girls, or both?"

Jonathan Kregel flopped on the chair near where he was standing. "Whew! You have no idea the anxiety I've allowed myself to feel since the Lord asked me to do this. I kept hearing him say, 'Peace, be still.' Yet, I was still uneasy." He laughed. "The twins are named after Tom's parents, Mark and Faith. Hannah felt they were the perfect examples of Christians and named her children after them. Of course, they were both dead before she had the twins."

Martha bit her bottom lip. "How old is everyone? I mean, what is the age of Hannah and the twins?" She paused. "When I was twenty-four, I had a dream that my daughter, Hannah was thirty-six, and my grandchildren were four."

Robert gasped. "You never told me that dream."

"I know, because I thought it was rather dumb for me to dream that my daughter is thirty-six when I was only twenty-four. I mean, it did seem ridiculous." She bit her bottom lip. "We'd only been married for a year, and it made no sense."

Pastor Kregel stood up. "Hannah is thirty-six and the twins are four." He clasped his hands together. "This is unreal. Of course, not when you know the Lord." He paused." God has been preparing you two for some time." He grabbed his head with both hands. "I'm not at all surprised." He paused. "Are you both telling me you want Hannah and the twins to come here?"

Robert Montgomery nodded his head. "I believe God is giving us the family he planned for us. That's why we never had children. If we had, we'd be involved with them and our grandchildren. This way, we can adopt them as our family." He scratched the back of his head with his left hand. "Several years ago, the Lord impressed that he's my Father through adoption. I didn't know why he said it, because I knew that." He chuckled. "Now, I understand. He was preparing me to be a father through adoption."

The pastor hugged him. "I really must get home, call Hannah, and tell her."

Martha pointed to the telephone. "You may call her from here. I mean, if we're to be a family, we better get to know one another."

She paused. "I mean, you do understand what I'm saying? Don't you?"

Robert nodded his head. "I agree with Martha. We'd better get to know her if she's going to live here."

"Yes. You're both right. Just give me a minute to pray for the words to say to her." He bowed his head. "Lord, please prepare Hannah's heart for this and give me the words to say. In Jesus' Name, Amen!"

"Amen!" Robert and Martha echoed.

He picked up the phone and called Hannah who was surprised to hear his voice on another unknown number. "Well, Pastor Kregel, how many phone numbers do you have?" Her voice trembled. "Does this mean you already have news for me? You just told me a bit ago to wait for your call."

The pastor chuckled. "Yes I have news for you." He paused. "This is not my number. It's the number of your new home."

"My what?"

"I'm trying to figure out how to say this, but a couple from the church would like to be your adoptive parents. It's a long story, but I know it's God's doing. As a matter of fact, this man is the one who the Lord's going to use to bring Tom back."

Hannah's voice trembled. "Pastor, I know it's God. You see, before my mother died, she said the Lord told her I was to be adopted by a couple who would be my other father and mother. She didn't want me to fight it, for it was his will for me and the twins." She paused. "I just figured it was her condition and went along with her. I'm just flabbergasted."

Robert Montgomery asked to speak with her. "Hannah, this is Robert Montgomery. My wife, Martha and I have been prepared by the Lord for this. We never had children. Anyway, we'll tell you everything after you get here." He paused. "Do you have the money to fly here?

"Yes, I have some money left from my mother's insurance policy."

"Okay. You just take your personal mementos. Don't worry about clothes or anything else. Just you and those children get here as soon as possible." He paused. "Oh yes, make sure you fly first class. We'll reimburse you whatever you spend."

"This is all so strange, but I was told by the Lord last week to pack all my keepsakes into a trunk ready to ship. He also told me to pack up suitcases for us to take a journey. I did it all. Anyway, all I need is the address to ship the trunk. I've some things I must handle. It'll take a couple of days, but I'll get the airline tickets right after I take care of things here." She paused. "Oh yes, I'll take a taxi to your house. I know what airports are like. It'll be easier all around, if we come there."

Robert gave her the address and prayed for them to have a safe journey.

Pastor Kregel was beside himself with elation. "I can't explain how delighted I am about this whole thing. I have no idea what's going on, but I have to calm my stomach down." He rubbed his bald head with his right hand. "Well, I better get to the church, I have some things to straighten out before our next board meeting." His face gave a quizzical look. "Robert, would you be interested in teaching the adult Sunday school class? I believe the Lord wants you to have the position." He paused. "It will be a few weeks, as I have it filled up until the third Sunday of next month."

He grabbed the pastor's right hand between his. "I've been praying to be used in teaching. I love being retired, but I truly miss teaching." He chuckled. "Of course, I'll remember I'm not Dr. Montgomery in the class, but Mr. Montgomery."

The pastor gave a questioning look. "You have a doctorate?"

"Yes, I have a PhD in theology. Once I started Bible College, I just inhaled it all. Before I knew it, I had earned a doctorate." His eyebrows scrunched together. "Why do you ask?"

"Dr. Steinberg helps do some counselling at the church, but he has his hands full at the company. After this thing with Tom is completed, would you consider counselling a couple of days a week?"

"Consider it, I accept. I've felt for some time the Lord wants me to counsel his people and help them to stay focused on the spiritual and not on the natural."

Pastor Kregel hugged him. "Well, Dr. Montgomery, welcome to my staff." He bit the hangnail on his right thumb. "I believe I'll introduce you as Dr. Montgomery in your Sunday school class. Some people may not be able to make the transition from Mr. Montgomery in Sunday school and Dr. Montgomery in a counselling session." He paused. "This way the degree of respect your education deserves will be given."

Chapter 5

Grandfather and Grandmother

LIKE CLOCK WORK, TOM showed up Thursday night pushing his squeaky cart with trash bags full of empty pop cans clanking against the sides of the cart. As usual, the neighborhood dogs down the street were barking at the racket.

Robert was sitting on the curb with several hamburgers, some apples, and bottles of iced tea on a tray beside him. As soon as Tom reached him, he said. "Tom, God has blessed us with a beautiful evening. Why don't you join me for hamburgers, some delicious apples, and iced tea? I truly don't want to eat alone."

Tom stopped, looked at the tray of food, reached down, emptied the tray taking one at a time with his right hand, and placing them in the front of his cart. He then continued pushing the noisy cart to the next house with a strategic movement that kept the flapping shoe from tripping up his momentum. Once Tom reached the next neighbor's house, Robert noticed he was eating a hamburger with his left hand while getting the cans into the bags with his right hand.

Martha joined her husband after Tom was out of sight. "Did he eat it? Did he drink? I mean, I saw him take them. Did you see what he did?"

"He took them all without even looking at me." He rubbed his chin with his right thumb and forefinger. "But I saw him eating a hamburger when he stopped at the house up the street." He shook his head. "This is really trying. I have to wait until next Thursday before I can do anything. I do need to seek the Lord. I find myself so attached to this young man. Everything in me wants to help him." He sighed. "It's only those who wait upon the Lord who have their strength renewed. As difficult as this is, I'll not run ahead of the Lord."

"Oh yes, Hannah and the children will be here Saturday morning at nine. She straightened out the things she told us about and booked the earliest flight. I told her we'd be waiting for her." She grabbed her face with both hands. "Robert, I can't get over how excited I am about all this. I mean, I know I'm sixty, but I feel like I've been her mother since I was twenty-four. It's like I expect her to look like my mother with blue eyes, black hair, about five foot two, and petite looking. Maybe I'm wrong, but it seems so strong that's what she looks like." She paused. "I mean, I can't wait until Saturday to see them."

"It's funny, but I didn't give any thought about her looks. I guess my mind's been on getting their rooms ready, and seeking the Lord about Tom." He scratched the back of his head with his left hand. "You know when the Lord told me to buy this 12,500 square foot house on eight acres, I thought I was hearing things. However, he was adamant about it. Praise the Lord I listened to him. Now, we'll have a bedroom for Hannah, Faith, Mark, and a play room for the children." He paused. "Plus, we still have four more bedrooms. That's not including what seems to be an efficiency apartment off the kitchen and that strange room near the pool."

Martha's face screwed up. "I know what you mean. Those rooms seem like extra. I mean, they seem as if they're not a part of the rest of the house. But they're in it."

He scratched the back of his head with his left hand. "I was thinking with the children, perhaps it's time to bring a couple into the quarters off the kitchen to cook, do the dishes, do laundry, etc. That way we'll be able to spend more time with the twins." He gestured with his left hand. "We don't need a maid or anything. I believe having the Maids-A-Clean on Tuesday and Friday is suffi-cient. The lawn care company does a good job. Plus, the pool people keep that up."

"I think you're correct. It would be nice not to worry about the cooking, dishes, or laundry. I mean, I've been doing it, but it would be lovely not to."

"Martha, I'm so sorry. It never entered my mind. I really should've made changes when I inherited all that money from my parents." He threw up his hands. "It's been multiplying when our life could have been easier."

Martha bit her bottom lip. "Robert, I was wondering if my sister would want to move in with us. She's only sixty-one, and you know she has a nursing degree. I mean, Mary always wanted chil-dren, but didn't have any. Perhaps, she could be the children's nurse or nanny. I mean, Mary doesn't have things too easy. When she sold the house, she had so many debts to pay off because of Pete's treat-ments. I know Pastor said he taught Sunday School, but he hadn't worked for almost five years." She paused. "That way if Hannah misses working, she could pursue her career in business adminis-tration. I mean, we'd have to ask them both what they think."

"I believe Hannah needs to pursue her career. I don't under-stand what's going on, but I believe you should ask Mary."

Robert and Martha were sitting on their porch in anticipation for Hannah's arrival. Martha was beside herself. "Oh, I do pray they take to us. I mean, I pray they look at us as family and not friends. I truly want to be her mother and their grandmother." She bit her bottom lip. "What do they call us? I mean, Hannah had a mom and dad. What can she call us?" She gazed into Robert's eyes. "The twins didn't know their grandfather, but they knew their grandmother. What can they call us? I mean, we really should know."

Robert touched her right knee with his left hand. "I believe the Lord has it all in hand. He's the one bringing this family together, so I think he's been talking to Hannah. It has to be something she can accept and be comfortable with." He paused. "If she's contented, it will make the transition easier."

"You walk in such wisdom. I mean, I hope the more I grow that I'll do the same."

"I pray for wisdom constantly. God gives wisdom liberally to his children who ask for it."

"Wow! I mean, I can ask for wisdom, and he'll give it to me. But don't I still have to get off the milk and onto the meat? I mean, doesn't maturity give you more wisdom?"

Robert held his wife's right hand with his left. "Martha, that was well said. Wisdom does come with maturity. However, if we lack wisdom in a situation, we ask God for it, and he'll give it to us."

"I'm asking right now for wisdom on how to be a good mother and grandmother. I have no idea how to be either. I mean, I have no experience."

"No, but you have experience on how to tend to people. As a nurse, you have dealt with young and old. As you seek God, he'll give you the ability to be what Hannah, Mark, and Faith need."

They were interrupted by a taxi pulling into their driveway. Martha jumped up and practically ran to the vehicle. Robert followed and went to the driver to pay him. "How much is the fare?"

"It's forty-three dollars and sixty cents."

He handed him a hundred dollar bill. The driver went to give the change. Robert shook his head. "You keep the change." He paused. "Now, if you give us a few minutes, we'll unload their belongings."

As Hannah stepped out of the taxi, Martha grabbed her face with both hands. "I'm so delighted. I mean, I knew you'd look like my mother. The Lord impressed me so strongly that you'd be a younger version of her." She gave her a hug and bent into the taxi to see the twins. "Oh my, look at those two darlings. I mean, they're so adorable."

They both took one of the twins out, while Robert unloaded the suitcases and put them on the side of the driveway where Martha, Hannah, and the twins were standing. Then they all stood in a row, as the driver backed out.

Hannah clasped her right hand to her heart. "I had no idea what to expect, but I have such feelings for you both already." Hannah's blue eyes sparkled and gleaned. "While in prayer, the Lord reminded me about my Mom saying I would have another father and mother. I believe he wants me to call you father and mother." She blushed. "Only if it's alright with you both."

Robert gave her a hug. "We're willing to be called whatever you're comfortable with. I know we'll not take the place of your Mom and Dad, but I pray you'll come to love us as your other parents."

Hannah's eyes filled with tears. "God has already done something in me. I can't explain it. It's like he ordained you both to be my parents and the twins grandparents." She grabbed Robert's right hand. "Thank you for being obedient to the Lord." She then grabbed Martha's left hand. "I thank you for being willing to do this." She cleared her throat. "Oh yes, the Lord said the children are to call you grandfather and grandmother." Her voice began to tremble. "Is that acceptable?"

Martha put her hands on her hips. "If that's what the Lord said, we aren't about to say different. I mean, we have no problem with any of it." She picked up Mark and gave him a kiss on his cheek. "Grandmother would like you all to come and have some lunch."

Robert nodded his head. "Yes, let's get inside. I'll carry the suitcases in. We'll have some lunch, get to know each other, and then we'll show you all to your rooms." He paused. "Some of the things ordered for the children's rooms should be here anytime. We've been waiting for the furniture delivery." He scratched the back of his head with his left hand. "If we've missed anything, please let us know what it is." He gestured to the suitcases. "Do you have enough clothes and things until Monday?"

"Yes. I also brought Sunday clothes. I don't want to miss church."

They had a leisurely lunch trying to get familiar with each other. Martha bit her bottom lip. "Hannah, I have a question to ask you. I mean, it's something important." She sipped her iced tea. "My sister is a registered nurse and is moving in with us."

Robert interrupted. "What Martha is trying to say is we both believe the Lord wants you to pursue business administration. Mary is willing to be the children's nurse/nanny, so you can do so."

Hannah's eyes filled with tears. "I really do miss it. It was most difficult working at the store." She gazed at Martha. "She's your sister?"

"Yes, she's a year older than me. She lost her husband recently, and they never had any children. She's always been a pediatric nurse. I mean, she loves working with children. As a matter of fact, she's really looking forward to it. She'll be moving in next week. She sold her house after Pete died, and moved into an apartment. Some of the nurses she worked with will be taking her furniture and things. I mean, she won't need anything but her personal belongings and clothes here."

"I'm really anxious to meet her. I've never had an aunt. Now, I have an Aunt Mary. This is all so exciting."

"Oh yes," Robert said, "the pool area is closed off and locked. I intend to make an area for the children that will be screened with a playset, a children's pool, etc." He paused, I was thinking of having someone teach them how to swim in our pool, and to teach them to never go near the pool without a life jacket on."

Martha bit her bottom lip. "Robert, I forgot to tell you I was talking to a woman who said her brother and his wife were teaching her children to swim. I mean, I believe they're swim instructors. She goes to our church, but I ran into her the other day at the grocery store." She paused. "I mentioned my excitement about Hannah and the twins. I mean, I told her that we had our pool locked to make it child safe. I told her they're only four, and I didn't think they knew how to swim." She gestured with both hands. "Anyway, she said her brother and his wife taught swimming lessons. I mean, I asked her if they would be willing to give private lessons in our pool."

Robert gestured with his left hand. "What did she say?"

"She said, yes. I mean, they only give private lessons."

Hannah cleared her throat. "Do you think they'd be willing to teach me? I've never learned myself."

Martha laughed. "I'm sure they'd be willing. I mean, if they give lessons, it must be all ages."

Mark gazed at Robert. "Are you my grandfather?"

"I believe I am."

"Could I sit on your lap?"

"If you'd like."

Mark climbed down from his booster seat, walked over to Robert, and reached up with both hands. Robert picked him up, and Mark placed both tiny arms around Robert's neck. "Grandfather, I love you."

Robert's eyes filled with tears. "And I love you, grandson."

At that, Faith climbed down from her booster seat, walked over to Robert, and reached up with both hands. "I love you too, grandfather. Can I sit on your other lap?"

Robert picked her up. She placed her tiny arms around his neck, kissed him on his cheek, and gave him a big smile. "I'm happy to be here."

Martha started to cry. "We're so happy to have you all here."

Faith cocked her head to her left. "Are you my new grandmother?"

"Yes, I am. I mean, if you want me to be."

Faith looked at Robert. "Grandfather could you help me down. I want to give grandmother a big kiss."

Before Robert could respond, Martha, with tears strolling down her cheeks, was up from her chair. As she picked Faith up, two little arms held fast around her neck. "I'm glad you're our grandmother." Her eyes widened as she looked around. "I love living in a castle." She pointed to Hannah. "Mommy didn't tell us our grandfather and grandmother lived in a castle." Her little eyebrows scrunched together. "Grandmother, are you a princess?"

"No, sweetie. I mean, we're just a grandmother and grandfather."

Mark got down from Robert's lap and walked over to Martha. "Can I give you a kiss, too?"

"Yes. I mean, you can kiss me anytime you want."

"I'm happy. I really am happy to be here."

Hannah's eyes teared up. "I must admit I'm happy to be here. I had no idea we'd live in such a place." She giggled. "It really does seem to be a castle." She cleared her throat. "Well, Father, I was wondering if you could tell me what's going on with Tom. Pastor Kregel said you're the one God is using to break through his grief."

Robert's eyes teared. "Whew! To hear me called father and grandfather is most joyous. I never thought we'd be parents, never mind grandparents." He paused. "I believe the Lord wants us to adopt you as soon as possible. There shouldn't be a problem, I'll see my lawyer Monday morning and it should all go smoothly." He scratched the back of his head with his left hand. "I believe the children are to remain as they are, because when you remarry, they'll be adopted."

Hannah's jaw dropped. "I believe that's what the Lord told me. Now, it's been confirmed." She giggled. "I don't have anyone in mind. My last experience has me walking very circumspectly."

Robert nodded his head. "Now, as for Tom, it's most distressing. He's in a dreadful state."

Martha interrupted. "He looks like one of those pictures we see of people in concentration camps. I mean, he's so skinny." She paused. "I'm so sorry, I interrupted you. I mean, I should've let you talk. He's so emaciated that its frightening."

"He is in a dreadful condition, but God told me to trust him. At first, I wanted to bring food to his cottage. However, the Lord told me to stay away from his safe haven, because he has to be there to be restored." He paused. "It's like his sanctuary at present, and we need to stay away. God knows how to reach him, and our good intentions could foul everything up."

"I never met him. He's a distant cousin. I believe his father was my mother's fourth cousin. My mother's maiden name was Nottingham, and her father was a third cousin to Tom's grandfather."

Martha's eyebrows scrunched together. "Okay, if that's the case, then Tom is your fifth cousin."

Robert nodded. "That sounds about right." He gave out a heavy sigh. "Anyway, I pray God intervenes in this situation. Tom really needs to get back from the dead into the land of the living."

"I've been praying for him since I've known about his situation. Lately, I've been feeling such a peace that God is moving. She paused. "How often do you see him?"

"That's the problem. I only see him on Thursday nights when he pushes his shopping cart to gather empty pop cans."

"What? He owns a big company. What's he collecting cans for?"

"We don't know why. He doesn't talk to anyone." He gestured with his left hand. "As a matter of fact, he doesn't even look at anyone. He obviously avoids eye contact."

"That's sad." She grabbed Robert's right hand. "Yet, there's such an expectation in me that God is moving in his life."

Robert rubbed his chin with his left thumb and forefinger. "Yes, I have the same expectation. Yet, I feel I haven't found the breach that will break through."

Hannah's voice trembled. "Perhaps it's not time. If the fulness of time was here, God would show you how to break through."

Robert chuckled. "I do believe I've allowed my emotions to cause me to become somewhat anxious." He paused. "I do believe I needed that." He hugged Hannah. "No matter how long we've served the Lord, we can allow ourselves to become anxious about things." He chuckled. "We become like Peter and look at the storm instead of keeping our eyes on Jesus."

"I know that all too well. After what happened, I almost sunk. My faith wavered so that I joined the disciples in the boat with a lack of faith. Once I took my eyes off the storm and placed them on God's word, I joined Jesus asleep in the boat."

Chapter 6

Employed Help

PASTOR KREGEL WAS DELIGHTED to finally meet Hannah and the children. "I can't tell you how pleased I am to have you all here." He gestured towards Tabitha. "My wife and I would love you all to join us for lunch. I know you probably have a lot of settling in to do. But if it's convenient, we'd appreciate your company."

Faith touched his right hand. "Pastor, we really don't have much to do." She gestured towards Robert and Martha. "Grandfather and grandmother do everything." She beamed. "They bought me a princess bed and all princess stuff for my room." Mommy didn't tell us that we were moving into a castle. I'm a princess living in a castle." She grabbed her face with both hands. "Mommy said it's all because of Jesus." She gave a heavy sigh. "I sure do thank Jesus for giving me grandfather and grandmother."

"Me too," said Mark. "I don't have princess stuff." His eyes widened. "I'm a pilot like the one on the plane when we came here." He hugged himself with excitement. "My bed's an airplane, and I have all kinds of stuff about airplanes." He threw up his hands. "Jesus really gave me the best grandfather and grandmother."

Jonathan's eyes teared. "He sure did." He gestured towards Robert and Martha. "They're both very special people." He gazed at Robert. "Will you all be able to join us for lunch?"

Robert nodded. "I really enjoy their food."

"As a matter of fact," Martha said. "We wish we could find a couple to cook. I mean, we'd like a couple who cook, take care of the dishes, the laundry, and serve us like a waiter."

Robert chuckled. "She means that we need to hire a couple to do what she said. However, I don't have a clue how to find such a couple."

The pastor grabbed his head with both hands. "God is awesome! This is incredible, but Jason and Leah Laurent would be the ideal couple." He paused. "I had invited them to join us yesterday when they helped clean the church. I'll let them tell you their story at lunch."

The Family Buffet was as crowded as ever, but Mr. Smith had the pastor's table reserved. As they all sat down, the Laurent's came in. Pastor Kregel introduced everyone. "Let's get our food, and we can have fellowship."

"I do believe I'm ready to eat," Robert said. "The aromas in here are causing my stomach to growl."

After things settled down a bit, the pastor addressed the Laurent's. "Jason and Leah, I don't want to embarrass you both, but Dr. Montgomery and Martha are looking for a couple who'd be willing to live in their house to do cooking, do dishes, do laundry, and be like a waiter at meal time." He rubbed his bald head with his right hand. "I know you're in a tight situation, would you consider such a position?"

Leah clasped her hands to her chest. "Pastor, we just prayed that last night. Jason is only fifty, but he's not been able to find a decent job since he lost his job at forty-two with Mulvaney's Restaurant. It seems the owner's son had just become a chef, and he wanted him in the position." Her eyes teared. "It didn't make sense that Jason couldn't find another chef's job. He's an excellent chef." She gestured with her right hand. "However, without his position, we lost the house, and moved into an efficiency room at the local motel. It's been difficult enough to pay for the room, our car payment, insurance, etc." She laughed. "When they let Jason go, they told me that they didn't need me as a waitress any longer."

Jason leaned forward. "I believe the devil meant to discourage us, but God kept us getting by these past eight years." He gestured with both hands. "It's been a struggle, but each month, we came through." He laughed. "It seemed every month we were in this dark tunnel. Yet God has taken us through to the light month after month."

Leah nodded her head. "It's like the Lord was preparing us for this."

"That's what I think," Jason laughed. "As a matter of fact, I'm looking forward to once again cooking fancy meals." His eyebrows scrunched together. "Dr. Montgomery, you will be wanting me to be a chef?"

Robert grabbed Jason's right hand between his. "You have no idea how delighted I am to have you both." He paused. "You won't have to do any other cleaning in the house. The kitchen is where you'll be. Of course, the breakfast room and the dining room will be included in the cleaning." He scratched the back of his head with his left hand. "The only other duty was the laundry. But as I was sitting here, I feel the Lord wants us to hire someone to live in to do laundry, make the beds, and do odds and ends cleaning that can't wait for the Maids-A-Clean on Tuesday and Friday."

Tabitha reached over and tapped Robert's right arm. "Excuse me, but I think I know the perfect person for that job. She works at the local motel. But after her husband past away last year, she's had things pretty tough. She's African-American, only forty-eight, childless, a devoted Christian, and a very good cook. Before her husband passed away, she had us over for dinner a few times." She paused. "Her name is Helen Reynolds."

Jason laughed. "It's a good thing we got hired first, or she'd be the cook." His face screwed up. "Seriously, though, perhaps she can cook on our days off."

Martha grabbed her face with both hands. "She could use the room near the pool that we couldn't figure what it was for. I mean, it seemed odd to have a room with a bathroom next to the pool. Yet, you can't get into it from the pool area. It's situated like it's not part of the house, yet it's off the area going out the backside of the house. I mean, it's sort of all by itself."

The pastor rubbed his bald head with his right hand. "Perhaps the people who owned it before you bought it had servants?"

"That's what we thought," Martha said. "It seemed odd to have what seemed to be an efficiency apartment off the kitchen. I mean, it's set up like one of those suites in a hotel with two bedrooms." She paused. "There's even room for a washer and dryer in the bathroom."

The Laurent's looked at each other. Jason gestured with his right hand. "Dr. Montgomery, when can we move in?" He paused. "Our rent at the motel is due again tomorrow."

Robert gestured with his hands. "Can you move in today?"

"We certainly can," Leah said. "We don't have much at the room." She gestured with both hands. "We only kept our bedroom set, a small table with two chairs, both our recliners, a round table that goes between them, and a few odds and ends in storage. We'll just rent a small U-Haul and empty it out. It shouldn't take more than a couple of hours to get it all."

Robert scratched the back of his head with his left hand. "Do you have the money to do this?"

"Yes," Jason said. "We won't have to pay rent, so we have sufficient."

Martha grabbed her face with both hands. "I forgot to tell you. You have a private entrance into your quarters. I mean, it's like your own apartment."

Robert laughed. "Well, that makes certain the people who sold us the house either had servants or had an in-law apartment." He paused and wrote on a piece of paper. "Here's the address and phone number. I don't have the keys to your entrance on me. But if you call us when you're pulling up to the house, I'll bring them out to you." Robert sat back in his chair. May I ask what you're expecting to earn at our house? Do you want a weekly amount or a monthly amount?"

"I'll take whatever you give me. I'm really tired of working part-time making burghers at the Burgher Shack." He gave a heavy sigh. "It's just after cooking fancy meals."

"Okay, I'll look into it and find out what a fair wage is." He chuckled. "I have no idea what to pay people."

Leah clasped her heart with both hands. "I just feel God wants us there, and that our wage is not important."

Jason nodded his head. "I believe the same. We'll have no more worries about rent or food." He shrugged his shoulders. "Our only concern will be our car payment and car insurance." He gestured with his right hand. "And whatever we personally need."

Robert rubbed his chin with his left thumb and forefinger. "Well, I'll pay off your car, and pay the insurance yearly. You'll also need health insurance. I'll get you the same plan we have." He chuckled. "Then I'm sure the Lord will show me a fair wage."

Leah threw up her hands. "Thank You Jesus!"

"Amen!" Pastor Kregel said. "I'm just beside myself that God moved the Montgomery's down here."

Robert and Martha were waiting for the Laurent's to call them. In the meantime, they were all playing hide and seek. Mark and Faith were to find their grandparents and their mother. It turned out to be quite a challenge for the little tykes, but they ventured through the house until they found them. Everyone was laughing when the telephone rang. Robert picked up the phone. "Hello!"

"Dr. Montgomery, this is Jason, we just pulled up in front of your house. Where do we pull in?"

"I'll be right out."

Robert brought out the keys to their quarters, showed them where to park, opened the door for them, beckoned them to enter, and handed Jason the keys. Both their jaws dropped as they entered the house. Jason grabbed Robert's right hand. "Dr. Montgomery, Mrs. Montgomery said this was like an efficiency apartment. I've never seen any look like this. This is like a house. It's quite fine."

"I'm pleased you like it." He paused, "Do you need any help bringing in your things?"

Jason laughed. "Dr. Montgomery, I think you have to get used to having servants." He blushed. "I'm sorry. I think that was disrespectful."

Robert chuckled. "My father owned Monti's Hardware chain. But he said never treat your employees as second-hand citizens. If you treat them as people, they'll respect you the more." He paused. "He always said they know where their bread is buttered, and will remain loyal."

Leah nodded her head. "That's wisdom. Your father must have loved the Lord."

"He did, but he didn't get saved until about a year after me. His father taught him that kindness will earn respect. After he was saved, he realized it was doing to others what you would have them do unto you." He scratched the back of his head with his left hand. "Well, I'll leave you two to do what you have to do." He paused. "We're about to grill some hamburgers, beef shish kebabs, and some shrimp skewers. Why don't you join us to eat? I'll let you know when it's ready."

Jason gestured with hands. "I thought I'm supposed to be the chef here. Why don't I do the cooking, and we can finish unloading after we eat?"

Robert gestured toward the door leading into the kitchen. "If you'll both follow me, I'll take you there."

Leah touched Robert's right arm. "You can all sit, and I'll serve. I'm really excited about this."

As they were led through the house, Jason and Leah gasped. It was Jason who spoke. "I had no idea we were going to live in such a palatial manor. This is almost unbelievable. If I wasn't awake, I would be convinced I was dreaming."

Leah just looked around as if in a daze. "I've never seen anything so beautiful in my life." She started to cry. "I can't thank God enough for this. I'm so humbled that he would bless us to live in such a mansion."

Robert rubbed his chin with his left thumb and forefinger. "The Lord just impressed me that you both have been faithful in a little, and now he's giving you more. Your life is to be much easier and enjoyable. I believe you are to have Sunday and Monday off." He paused. "I do believe we'll have Helen cook on your days off, and give her Tuesday and Wednesday off." He chuckled. "I sense this is going to improve the quality of life for all of us.

Chapter 7

God Makes the Family

ROBERT VISITED HIS LAWYER first thing Monday morning. "Well, Robert," James Fields said, "What brings you to my office?"

"It's rather a long story, but I'll try to give a synopsis. It seems that God is giving Martha and me a family. We are about to adopt a thirty-six year old young woman named Hannah." He scratched the back of his head with his left hand. "Well, James, it's a good thing you're a Christian. You see, God told us to adopt her and bring her and her four-year-old twins to live with us. Apparently, her mother told her it would happen before she passed away." He rubbed his chin with his left thumb and forefinger. "Is there any way to get this done without a hassle? It's not like we have to deal with parental rights or anything. Hannah is in agreement with Martha and me about the adoption."

James shook his head and grinned. "It just so happens I'm having lunch at one this afternoon with Judge Morris. He's an old school buddy, and we've been friends for over thirty-five years. If something can be done to speed things along, he'll know what to do." He paused. "Do you have all the necessary information?"

"I believe I have all the material from Hannah. However, what I don't know, I'll call and get from her."

"Okay, I'll have my secretary get straight to the court house and get the necessary papers." He left his office and quickly returned. "Well, she shouldn't be too long." He sat back in his chair. "In the meantime, you can tell me what's been going on. I was supposed to be in court this morning, but it was postponed." He chortled. "God is awesome! He knew you'd be here, and I needed to be free."

Robert told him about Thomas Nottingham and how the Lord wanted him to be the Good Samaritan to Tom. "I've been beside myself about what to do. But I know God is in control, so I'll just take each Thursday night according to his leading."

"Oh my! I knew his father quite well, but not the son. I wasn't their lawyer. Philip Jenkins is a business lawyer, so he handles their company." He paused. "I believe he mentioned something about the son losing his family in an accident, but I didn't know about his condition." He looked at his watch. "Philip lives quite a ways from here in the country. It seems he and his wife don't like the hustle of the city. However, he can't avoid it with his business." He chortled. "Our paths hardly ever cross."

As soon as the secretary returned with the papers, they wasted no time filling them out. Robert was pleased to have everything finished and notarized before lunch. "Thank God it's done." He paused. "Now, we just wait for a court date."

James gathered up his briefcase, and paused. "On second thought, why don't you join us for lunch. It's not about legal business, it's just our Monday lunch that we try to have weekly."

"Okay. I think I'd like that."

Robert was surprised to find they met at the Family Buffet. "I can't believe this. We've been coming here on Sunday's after service."

"Really? I wonder why we haven't seen each other?" He chortled. "Marian and I come here after Church." He hit his forehead with his right hand. "Where's my thinking? We've missed the past three weeks, because we were on vacation. We didn't get home until after midnight last night." He yawned. "I guess I'll catch up on my sleep tonight."

As they sat down, Judge Morris came in. "There's Adam now." He waved to show Adam where he was sitting. When he came over to the table, James gestured towards Robert. "Judge Morris, this is Dr. Montgomery." He grinned. "I do believe we'd do better if we call each other by our first names." He gestured towards Robert with his right hand. "Adam, this is Robert."

The judge laughed and put out his hand. "Glad to meet you Robert. If James has you here, there must be a personal reason."

James motioned with both hands. "Let's get our lunch, and I'll fill you in on the details."

After they'd settled down with their lunch, James brought the judge up-to-date about the adoption. The judge clasped his hands together. "That's wonderful. God never ceases to amaze me." He paused. "You said you have all the necessary papers together?"

"Yes, we did them this morning." He shrugged his shoulders. "I didn't know if you could move things along. I know it's no big deal with the Montgomery's adopting Hannah to take care of her and her twins, but Robert senses it's to be done promptly."

"I'll see what I can do to set up a hearing as quickly as possible." He tapped his lips with his right forefinger. "I believe God is in on this, so I expect things to go quickly. I'll look into it this afternoon."

Robert was pleased they only had to wait two weeks for the court date. He, Martha, Hannah, and the twins were there and waiting for the judge to come in. Robert was so pleased to see Adam. "I'm glad it's you that'll be handling this. This way, things will be easier."

Adam smiled. "It seems there was a postponement of another case, and I asked them to put this in its place." He shook Robert's hand. "It's a privilege to meet your family."

There were the usual questions, and it was over in about half an hour.

Hannah clasped both hands to her heart. "Thank you, Judge. I'm overjoyed to be adopted by these two wonderful people. It's only been a few weeks, but I feel as though they've always been my father and mother. When God makes the family, it's like it's always been." Her voice trembled. "I'll always love my mom and dad, but it seems I was meant to be Hannah Montgomery." She cleared her throat. "I don't think I'm getting this across properly."

Judge Morris smiled. "When God is in something, it just seems natural."

"Yes! That's what I was trying to say."

The judge addressed Robert and Martha. "The both of you are special people. Ever since Robert told me about this adoption, I knew it was God's doing." He bowed his head. "Father, I pray you bless this couple and mold this family into a special union. In Jesus Name, Amen!"

"Amen!" Robert, Martha, and Hannah responded in unison.

Martha bit her bottom lip. "This has to be one of the happiest days of my life. I mean, the happiest was when I accepted Jesus. But this is just overwhelming. I mean, I'm officially a mother to this wonderful girl, and I'm grandmother to these special little ones." Her eyes filled with tears. "God is so good!"

Hannah gave her a hug. "I'm pleased to be able to call you Mother." She hugged Robert. "And I'm grateful to call you Father."

Tears strolled down Robert's cheeks. "I couldn't have asked for a more special daughter and grandchildren." He threw up his hands. "Thank you, Jesus for my special family."

Mark looked at the judge. "Judge, do you know that my grandfather bought us a playset with a house on top, swings, slide, and things?"

"Did he now? I guess you like your grandfather."

Faith's face gave a scowl. "We love our grandfather."

The judge laughed. "I meant that you like what he's doing for you."

Faith smiled. "Yes, we do."

Mark tapped the judge on his back. "We love grandmother too. She does so many things with us."

Judge Morris stood up. "I do believe this is one of the happiest things I've done as a judge." He shook Robert's hand. "Robert, I'm pleased to know you." He paused. "Oh yes, Pastor Kregel said you'll be teaching the adult Sunday school class. My wife and I have decided to go back to Hope Tabernacle. We were going to the church five minutes from our house. It takes over forty-five minutes to get to Hope, but we really miss Pastor Kregel's sermons." He laughed, "Now, we'll be in your class."

Robert scratched the back of head with his left hand. "Well, I'll see you in Sunday school." He gave the judge a hug. "Again, thank you for making this such a blessed day." His eyes filled with tears. "I understand what Hannah meant. It seems she's always been my daughter, and Mark and Faith have always been my grandchildren." He paused. "What an awesome God we serve." His voice shook. "Because He makes the family, it becomes so special. My heart is delighted."

Chapter 8

The Breach

ROBERT WAS DETERMINED TO bring Tom back from the dead or darkness he'd been chained in for about three years. He prayed for God to show him what to do. Each Thursday, he would put out what the Lord told him to feed Tom. However, each week, Tom would stop, avoid looking at Robert, take the sandwiches, the fruit, the drinks, and continue up the street with his cart.

It had been five weeks since he started this Good Samaritan routine, but he felt he was making no headway with Tom. "Lord, please help me to reach this man. How can I cause a breach in his cocoon he's enclosed himself in? There must be something I can do to penetrate through it. How can I cause his wall to crumble?" He sat quietly at his desk with his head resting on his arms.

He was interrupted by a small hand tugging on his arm. "Grandfather, what's a breach?" Faith's green eyes looked up at him. "Did you mean you want the beach in his cocoon?"

Robert picked her up and gave her a big hug. "My little darling, I believe the Lord just used you to help me." He put her on his lap. "A breach is something that puts a hole in a wall." He chuckled. "Anyway, it's the gap I need to help someone I've grown very fond of. And I believe God just showed me how."

"You mean the man that pushes the noisy shopping cart, and you give him food?"

"Yes, that's what I mean."

Mary came to the door. "I was helping Mark with his puzzle. When I turned around, Faith was gone. I'm sorry, I told them both not to go in your study."

Faith eyes widened. "Aunt Mary, you said when grandfather wasn't in here." She pointed to Robert. "But he's sitting right here."

Mary shook her head. "Yes, I did, but it would be best if you didn't come in here unless your grandfather asks you."

Robert put her down. "Well, I do believe the Lord just used her to show me something that I've been praying about." He gave Faith a kiss on her forehead. "I think you need to go with your aunt. I have some things to see to. I'll see you at dinner."

She reached up with her tiny arms and hugged his neck. "Thank you grandfather for telling me what a breach is." She stood tall. "Now, I can tell Mark what it is."

Robert chuckled. "Yes, you can." He paused. "Mary would you tell Martha and Hannah I need to see them directly?"

She nodded her head and took Faith's left hand. "I'll go tell them now."

The next Thursday, Robert believed he had his breach ready. As soon as he heard the squeaky cart down the street, he had Martha, Hannah, Mark, and Faith all sit down on the curb with him. This time he had a few pizzas and ginger ale. He could feel his stomach fluttering with the anticipation. Taking a few deep breaths. "Now, everyone must do what we've been planning. Mark and Faith, I'm really counting on you to do only what I told you to do."

Mark beamed. "Mommy told us he's our only cousin, and he's a very sad man." He touched his mother's arm. "She said we have to help him be happy."

Faith nodded her head. "Grandfather, we want to see this man happy." She crossed her heart. "I promise, I'll only say and do what you told me to."

"Me too," Mark said, crossing his heart. "I promise to do what you told me to do."

Hannah's voice trembled. "I don't believe I've ever been more nervous, but I've been praying about this. I do believe tonight is the night of the breach. Exactly what it means or how it's to be done, I have no idea. All I know is I'm feeling this profound expectation."

Robert scratched the back of his head with his left hand. "That's exactly what I'm feeling. I'm beside myself with expectancy. I could hardly sleep after the Lord gave directions to make the breach."

Martha nodded her head. "Same here. I mean, I'm also feeling such anticipation."

Robert put his left forefinger to his lips. "Hush! Not another word. He's almost here."

As usual, Tom was bent over, keeping strategic movement with his shoe, and pushing the squeaky cart with trash bags full of empty cans clanking against the sides. For some strange reason, the dogs down the street were silent. Robert wondered if this was a sign from the Lord. Anyway, he gave out a heavy sigh as the cart approached. "Tom, it's so good to see you. I want you to meet my family, have pizza, and pop with us." He motioned with his hand to his right side. "This is my wife, Martha, my daughter, Hannah, and my grandchildren, Mark and Faith."

Robert saw Tom's body tremble at the names of his grandchildren. "Please join us for pizza. You can sit between Mark and Faith." Again, Tom's body trembled.

Mark stood up and touched Tom's right arm. "I'm Mark, and I'm glad to meet you."

Next, Faith stood up and touched his right arm. "I'm Faith, and I'm so happy to meet you."

At that, Tom's head came up over his right arm. When he looked up, Robert offered him a box of pizza and a pop. For the first time, Tom's eyes caught Robert's eyes. Then he caught sight of Mark. Breathing heavily and trembling, he quickly grabbed the pizza, the pop, and put them into his cart. As he pushed the cart away, his body was trembling so much that he almost tripped over the flapping shoe.

Robert motioned for everyone to be silent and stay sitting. Once Tom was out of sight, he motioned for them all to go into the house. "I think we'd better go in. I need to talk to the Lord about what happened."

Martha bit her bottom lip. "Robert, something happened. I mean, his whole body was trembling. I don't think he's done that before."

Robert shook his head. "No, I'm believing God that we had a breach in his cocoon tonight."

Hannah's blue eyes sparkled. "I'm sure something happened. When I saw his eyes look at you, I felt this elation that I can't explain."

"Grandfather," Faith said. "I thought you said a breach is a hole. I didn't see any hole in that man."

Everyone started to laugh. Robert picked her up. "It's not a hole in the person, but a hole in his cocoon of sadness that he's imprisoned in."

Mark's nose scrunched up. "Why didn't you unlock his prison door, then?"

Hannah cleared her throat. "I think what grandfather is trying to say is the man is very sad, and we were trying to find a way to make him happy."

"Thank you for that explanation." Robert chuckled. "I really do need to figure a way to talk to them at their level and not at mine."

Faith kissed his cheek. "I like how you talk. Besides, I want to be smart like you."

He put her down as Mary came out to help get the children in. While Martha and Hannah took in the pizza and pop. Martha shook her head. "What are we going to do with this pizza? I mean, I certainly don't want to spoil our dinner."

Mark and Faith both jumped up and down. "Can we eat it? Please? Please? We love pizza."

Mary gestured towards Hannah. "If your mommy says it's okay, it's fine with me."

"It's fine with me. After they eat, they can go and play in their playroom." She giggled. "That way, we can have a chance to talk about things."

Mary's eyebrows scrunched together. "I think I'll take care of feeding them supper at four-thirty, get their baths, and have them in bed by six-thirty. I've had a problem with them being up so late. Children need sleep. I do believe that's why they can never finish dinner and are falling asleep." She paused. "I'm not trying to control things, but seven is late for children to have dinner. By rights, they should be in bed before that."

"Yes," Hanna said. "I believe you're correct. I've read that children ages three to five should have ten to thirteen hours of sleep a night for proper growth." She cleared her throat. "I don't consider you taking control, but doing what you came here to do. You're the professional, and I accept your advice."

Mary took the pizza with her right hand, took Faith's right hand with her left hand. "Mark, you take your sister's left hand, and we'll go into the breakfast room for you to eat your pizza." She gazed at the adults. "If you'll all excuse me, I'll get them fed, bathed, and in bed. Then I'll be ready for dinner at seven."

As Mary and the children walked away, Martha put her hands on her hips. "This way we can make dinner more formal. I mean, we can enjoy our meal in the dining room without interruptions."

"This is beginning to feel like gentry." Hannah giggled. "It really will be nice to have dinner with just us adults." Her voice trembled. "I didn't mean anything negative about my children. But I believe this is the time we all have to get together, and we have to watch what we say around the children. They're so inquisitive and question just about everything."

Robert nodded his head. "Yes, there are many things I'd like to talk about at dinner, but not in front of the children." He scratched the back of his head with his left hand. "Thank God for Mary." He paused. "Besides, it'll be good for her to sit down and eat without being concerned with the children."

Martha bit her bottom lip. "Yes, dinner should be a time for us to talk about things. I mean, we're busy all day. Now, we can take our time eating and have adult fellowship."

"I think I'll tell Jason and Leah," Robert said. "This way they'll be aware of what's going on and not be concerned about the children's eating." He paused. "The only problem is how will Mary prepare their dinner without interrupting Jason?"

Jason laughed. "Dr. Montgomery, this kitchen is set up in such a way that a few people could be cooking at the same time. That's why I'm convinced the previous owners had a good size staff. I'll show Mary where she can work without interfering with me." He paused. "Besides, she'll be in here early, if the children are to eat at five."

Robert scratched the back of his head with his left hand. "I just didn't want you to be hindered." He chuckled. "You are truly a magnificent chef. God has really blessed us with you two."

Leah's eyes teared. "I believe the Lord has truly blessed us with you. Our life is unstressed."

"Amen!" Jason said. "We have spent so many years in constant stress. I believe the Lord allowed it until we could come here." He rubbed the back of his neck with his right hand. "If I hadn't lost my job and unable to find another suitable, we would still be living in our house." He laughed. "What I'm trying to say is that even though we had a decent job and home, it was still full of stress. This is so rewarding. I get to do what I love without any worries of keeping up the payments, etc." He gave Robert a hug. "Dr. Montgomery, we can't thank the Lord enough for you and your family." He laughed. "It's like we're on a permanent vacation."

Leah shook her head. "We feel like we're living at a resort. The food is unbelievable, we have fantastic quarters, we get to use the pool every day." She threw up her hands. "We're incredibly blessed."

Chapter 9

Restoration

INSIDE THE COTTAGE, THOMAS Nottingham sat on the floor in a corner of the living room staring at the family picture of himself, his wife, and children sitting on the fireplace mantle. His eyes were blank as if devoid of feeling. He was a man in severe grief who had lost touch with his emotions.

Suddenly, he got up and went into his bedroom, opened the closet door, took a box down from the shelf, and went back to sit in his corner of the living room. At first, he just stared at the box, rubbing his left arm with his right hand. He gave out a heavy sigh and opened the top, stared into the box, and again sat rubbing his left arm with his right hand. Then he reached in, pulled out a picture album, and placed it on his lap. Once again, he leaned back against the wall while rubbing his left arm with his right hand.

His eyes suddenly focused on the Bible on the coffee table. Again, he stared as if devoid of feeling. As he glared, he started to tremble, until he sat hugging himself. Then with a robotic motion, he opened the picture album, looked down at the pictures on the page, again began to tremble, hugged himself, and rocked back and forth.

Once more, with a robotic motion, he turned the page, looked down at the pictures on the page. Only this time, a tear started to develop in his right eye, his lips started to quiver, and he cried out as if in great pain. "God, I begged you to take me, but I'm still here. I want to be with my wife and kids. I have nothing here. You took them all." He looked up to Heaven. "I always thought you loved me, but how can this be love?" He fell sideways on the floor. "God, I know I was wrong to be more concerned about losing the business to the neglect of my family. But I didn't want them to go through what we did when my father lost his business."

Suddenly, there was a sound outside his door. Thomas jumped up and peaked out the window of the door. He had to blink his eyes several times. "What's that dog doing here?" He opened the door and a toy poodle ran in. At first, Thomas was going to forbid it, but something inside him wanted it to come in. "Well, little fellow, you seem to be hungry. I don't think you can have pizza, but it does have sausage on it. Perhaps you can have some of the crust without the sauce and some sausage. I'll cash in my cans tomorrow and buy you some dog food." He picked the dog up, and it licked his face. "I know what loneliness feels like. It can be quite depressing, but I think God wants me to have you or you to have me." His face screwed up. "Either way, how on earth did you get over that fence? I know you couldn't have squeezed through the two-inch spacing."

Tom busied himself with getting the dog something to eat, and took a bowl down from the cupboard and gave him some water. "You remind me of black Sambo. I used to read that story to my children." He stood still and rubbed his left arm with his right hand. "Why did that man look like my father? He had his eyes, his hair color, and resembled him in size and manner."

He began to tremble. "Those children. The boy resembled my dad when he was young. Lord, what's going on? What's this all about?" He gazed down at himself and gasped. "How did I get so skinny. My clothes are falling off me." He reached down and picked up the dog who immediately licked his face. "I think I'll call you Sambo."

He carried the dog into the living room, and sat back in his corner. "What did I do? How did I get so skinny?" He jumped up and went into his bedroom, opened his closet, pulled out a pair of jeans, a shirt, and reached up and got a pair of sneakers from the shelf. He sat down on the bed and whimpered. "God, I'm so humiliated. I've been walking around like this." He grabbed his head with both hands. "Why has that man been so friendly to me? I'm a sight for sore eyes. How did this happen?"

He was interrupted as Sambo jumped up on his bed and started to lick his face. "Sambo," he said through quivering lips, "I'm so ashamed." As the words came out of his mouth, he heard in his spirit. "I'll never leave thee nor forsake thee. I am the Lord that healeth thee."

At that he fell prostrate on the floor. "Jesus, you've been here with me through it all. I'm so sorry for ignoring you. I guess I was blaming myself for their death. Jonathan always taught nothing happens without God's permission." He got up, went to his bureau, pulled out his diary. "Lord, you told me that I was going to go through a dark time, that you'd be with me through it all, and that you'd heal me. And after I came through, the light would shine as the noonday sun." Tears streamed down his cheeks. "That was the dark time, and you've been with me through it all, and I'm healed." He looked around the room. "Is Sambo the light shining as the noonday sun?"

As he sat there, he heard his stomach growling. "Lord, I think I'm hungry. I must have been eating. How else could I be alive." He grabbed his head with both hands. "I don't even know what year it is." He paused. "Wait a minute, I have a computer in the other bedroom." He quickly went into the other room, turned on his computer, and almost fainted. "My God, it's been about four years since they died. The last thing I remember is going to Hawaii on vacation. I think I remember going to Arizona after that. How long have I been back? I seem to remember living in the woods in a small cave. Where was it? When did I leave it? How long have I been here? I only remember that man talking to me for a few weeks." He grabbed his head with both hands. "Lord, I feel like King Nebuchadnezzar who just came back from years of insanity." He rubbed his left arm with his right hand. "What about the company? They must all think I'm dead." His eyes teared. "Lord, it's like I'm back from the dead. I've been restored." He paused. "Lord, what do I do? Do I go to that man's house?" He rubbed his left arm with his right hand. "I sense that man is part of your future will for my life."

Early Friday morning, Tom showered and put on the clean clothes. He looked in the mirror. "They're practically falling off me, but at least they're clean." He picked up his old shoes. "How on earth was I walking in these?" He grabbed his head with both hands. "Lord, thank you for not leaving me. How else could I still be alive. I don't remember eating, drinking, sleeping, or how I got back here." He rubbed his left arm with his right hand. "Father, I need grace to go to that man's house. Please help me." He gestured towards Sambo. "I don't want to leave him alone. Do you think it would be all right if I take him?"

He picked up Sambo, made a harness out of a pillow case, and pinned a piece of rope to it. "Now, Sambo, I guess it's time for us to meet that man who looks like my father."

As they approached the house, Tom could feel his heart pounding against his chest. He took a deep breath. "Lord, I know I can do all things through Christ which strengtheneth me. Please help me to do this." He walked up the steps to the porch and rang the doorbell.

Robert happened to be heading to the porch to get his morning paper as the doorbell rang. When he opened the door and saw Tom, he immediately hugged him. "Tom, it's you. Come on in." He paused. "What do you have there?"

Tom's mouth quivered. "This is Sambo? I found him outside my door last night."

Robert's eyebrows scrunched together. "How did he get over the fence?"

Tom shrugged his shoulders. "I have no idea. He's obviously a gift from the Lord."

"Tom, I'm elated to see you." He shook his head. "You're talking and acting normal." He threw up both arms. "Thank you, Jesus!"

Tom's eyes filled with tears. "He's been with me through it all." He rubbed his left arm with his right hand. "I have no idea how I've survived. I don't even know how I got back here. I left about three years ago for Hawaii, and then I went to Arizona." He gestured with both hands. "That's the end of my memory." He put his right hand on Robert's left shoulder. "Last night when I looked into your eyes, I saw my father. You have an incredible resemblance to him."

Robert chuckled. "That's what Pastor Kregel told me. He was certain that's why God told me to be the Good Samaritan to you." He scratched the back of his head with his left hand. "You seem to be completely healed. This is amazing."

"I told the Lord I feel like King Nebuchadnezzar coming back from insanity. It's like the Lord has brought me back from the dead and completely restored my mind." He gestured with his hands towards his body. "Now, I have to bring this back."

"Well, why don't you join my family and me for breakfast. Our chef should have it ready by now."

"If it wouldn't be an inconvenience, I'd be happy to join you." He picked up Sambo. "What do I do with Sambo?"

"Bring him in. I'm sure Mark and Faith will love him."

Tom rubbed the back of neck with his right hand. "I thought they said they were Mark and Faith." His eyes filled with tears. "My parents were named Mark and Faith."

"I know. I think you have a little surprise coming. I'll let Hannah tell you the story."

When Robert walked into the breakfast room, the others were seated. Martha screeched. "Thomas Nottingham. It's you." She ran over and gave him a hug. "I knew there was a breach last night. I mean, I didn't expect such a miracle to happen this fast."

Robert introduced everyone to each other. Mark looked at Tom with quizzical eyes. "Does this mean you're no longer sad but happy. That's what mommy said we needed to do."

Faith nodded her head. "After all, mommy said we should do all we can to make our cousin happy."

"Cousin? What do you mean. I don't have any cousins."

Hannah cleared her throat. "My mom was Grace Nottingham, your father's distant cousin." Her voice trembled. "These two people have adopted me and brought me and my children to live here."

Tom gazed at Mark. "That's why he looks like my father when he was a child. He's family." Tears streamed down his face. "I didn't know I had any family left."

Martha noticed the makeshift harness and leash. "Tom, we lost our little dog, Hobbit, a couple of years ago. We couldn't get rid of his harnesses and leashes. I mean, I'd like you to have one for your dog." She paused. "What's his name?"

"Sambo. He just reminded me of little black Sambo. He seemed so brave the way he came into the cottage. It was like his clothes were gone to keep predators from harming him." He laughed. "I know he's a dog. But when I saw him come in, I saw the children's book I read to my children when they were young." He shrugged his shoulders. "I believe the Lord wanted me to name him that."

She gestured with her right forefinger and left the room.

Mark got down from his booster seat and came over to Sambo. "May I pet him?" Before Tom could respond, Sambo jumped up on Mark who fell down backwards on the floor. Immediately, the dog was on top of him licking his face.

Tom laughed. "I think it's fine with Sambo."

Hannah clasped both hands to her heart. "This is all so wonderful." She went over and gave Tom a hug. "I've been praying for you ever since we learned what happened." Her blue eyes teared. "God is awesome." She gestured with her hands. "To see you standing here, talking, and being normal is a miracle."

Tom looked into her eyes. "I believe the Lord has completely restored me. It all happened last night." He gestured towards Robert. "When I saw his eyes and hair, it was like seeing my father. Then when I heard the names of Mark and Faith, something started to happen. Especially, when I saw Mark looked like my father as a young child."

Before he continued, Robert touched his shoulder. "Let's sit down and have breakfast, and we can continue to talk."

They all sat down at the table, and Martha returned with the harness and leash. "I think this one will fit. We have several others, and later you can choose which ones you want. I mean, we have more of this size." She paused. "May I put this on him?"

Tom nodded his head. "Please do." He gave a heavy sigh. "Anyway, as I was sitting in the cottage, I suddenly remembered the pictures in my closet. At first, I didn't know what was going on. I saw my father's picture and it resembled Robert. However, the picture of my father about Mark's age could have been his twin." He rubbed his left arm with his right hand. "Then I heard a sound at my door, and found Sambo at it." He laughed. "After that, I believe the Lord restored my mind and healed my grief." He gestured at his body with both hands. "I have no idea how I became so skinny. I don't feel sick or anything."

Robert chuckled. "Well, we'll get you fattened up. Especially with our chef's cooking."

At that Leah and Jason came into the room with their breakfast. Jason stopped mid-stride at seeing another person sitting at the table. "If you'll give a minute, I'll get another plate for your guest."

Robert gestured at Tom. "This is Thomas Nottingham, and we need to help fatten him up."

Jason laughed. "No problem. I'll be back with double portion for him."

Faith tilted her head and stared at Tom. "You sure are skinny. I guess that's why grandfather was giving you food." Her little nose screwed up. "Grandfather said we had to make a breach in your cocoon. I thought it was hole, but Mommy said it meant that you were very sad, and we had to make you happy."

Tom clenched his lips to refrain from laughing. "Your grandfather is a very wise man."

Mark held his chin high. "That's because grandfather asks Jesus what to do. He said Jesus told him we had to make a breach in your cocoon, so Jesus could make you happy."

"That's a correct analogy," Tom said. "I was imprisoned in my grief. It seemed the more I blamed myself for their death, the deeper into oblivion I went." He rubbed his left arm with his right hand. "It was as if last night, I entered sanctuary. The presence of God was able to break through." He laughed. "All I know is I was shocked to find it'd been three years since I left on a vacation to Hawaii. I lost track of time." He gestured with both hands. "To be honest, I don't know how I started collecting the cans. How did I know what day to pick them up?" He paused. "It had to be the Lord. He told me last night that Robert was part of what He has planned for my future."

Mary reached over and touched his right hand. "Tom, if my husband hadn't been sick for so long before he died, I'm not sure what the grief would've done to me." Her lips quivered. "Although it still hurts, I knew God was taking him home."

Helen bit the inside of her right cheek. "May I say something?"

Tom nodded. "Yes, of course."

"After my husband's funeral, I closed myself in my bedroom for over a week. I couldn't eat. I felt so alone. It was like his pillow still held his presence, and I didn't want it to go away." She pressed her lips together. "When I missed church, Pastor Kregel was at my house on Monday afternoon. At first, I didn't answer the door, but he kept ringing the doorbell. When I opened the door, he immediately went into prayer. He bound the spirit of depression that was trying to consume me." Her eyes teared. "He had me go with him to the Family Buffet for lunch." She gestured with both hands. "You lost all your family without warning. I knew my husband was dying for months. Pastor Kregel got me the job, and had me move into another apartment. Yes, it was still difficult, but I knew Jacob was out of pain and with Jesus."

Tom patted her right hand. "The problem with me was that I allowed the heaviness of worry about the business weigh me down. I know that worry, fear, anxiety, etc. are all weights that will lead to a lack of faith." He bit his top lip. "I leaned on my own understanding, instead of faith. When that happened, I supported what I did on my understanding, my logic, etc. and not faith in God and his word." He gave out a heavy sigh. "I didn't trust God enough to lead me in how to keep the business afloat. Instead, I worked late nights and weekends trying to control everything. I did this at the neglect of my family. Then when the accident took place, I blamed myself." He gestured with both hands. "As if I'm the giver and taker of life." He sat back and laughed. "Praise the Lord for his faithfulness!" He paused. "He told me all about everything before it happened."

Martha's eyebrows scrunched together. "How did he do that? I mean, what do you mean he told you about it all before it happened?"

"He told me I was going to go through a dark time, he'd be with me through it all, and he'd heal me. After it was over, he said the light would shine as the noonday sun."

Hannah's jaw dropped. "Wow! That's the Lord I love and serve. I, too, went through a dark time, he was with me through it all, and he healed me." Her voice trembled. "Being here as Hannah Montgomery is definitely the light at the end of the tunnel for me."

"I have to say the same thing," Mary said. "Living here is overwhelming with joy. I miss my husband, but God has filled my life with so much light with the care of these two children."

Helen pressed her lips together. "I feel like I'm a princess living in a castle. I never thought I'd have such a life. All worries of finances are gone. I have plenty of food, the house is beautiful." She gestured with both hands. "Plus, I get to take a nightly swim in the pool before bed. I feel as though I'm on vacation and not employed." She pressed her lips together. "It's difficult to explain. All I know is I can't thank God enough for the Montgomery's and their kindness."

Tom leaned forward. "I do believe God brought me back from the dead and completely restored me like he did King Nebuchadnezzar."

"Well," Jason said, carrying a plate full of food, "I do believe this breakfast is the start of plumping you up."

Tom's eyes bulged. "Wow! I hope I can eat all of that." He paused. "Now that I think of it, outside of a little sausage and crust for Sambo, I ate all that pizza last night without any difficulties."

After breakfast, Robert sat back and folded his arms. "Tom, there's some people who'll be praising the Lord when they see you." He paused. "We won't tell anyone what's happened. If you wouldn't mind staying here, I believe you should just relax today and eat. Tomorrow, we'll get you some clothes that fit. Then, on Sunday, we'll all go to church together."

Mark interrupted. "Do you know how to swim? Grandfather is having Bill and Delores teach me, Faith, and Mommy how to swim in his big pool."

Tom nodded. "Yes, I know how to swim, but I haven't done so in a while." He laughed. "I was on the swim team in college. I've always loved to swim." He gestured with his right hand. "I'd be happy to stay here. I think I've spent too much time alone."

Faith beamed. "Does that mean Sambo will stay here too?"

Robert chuckled. "Yes, Sambo will stay here also."

Chapter 10

Light Shines as the Noonday Sun

ROBERT HAD TOM GET some every day clothes, a couple of Sunday suits, a couple of swim trunks, underwear, socks, etc. The salesman who helped was able to show them clothes that took away some of the gaunt look in Tom. "Well, Tom, what a difference these clothes have made. It shouldn't be too long, and you'll have to replace these for a larger size." He chuckled. "I think Jason is going to work overtime to fatten you up some."

"As soon as I get my affairs straightened, I'll pay you back."

"There'll be no need for that. You have no idea how full my heart is at seeing you restored to a normal life." He paused. "I think on the way back home, I'm to tell you the story about Hannah and the twins."

After Robert finished the story of Hannah, Tom's eyes filled with tears. "How did she cope with such a shock? I did wonder where the children's father was." He grabbed his head with both hands. "She has a degree in business administration. That's impressive." He paused. "I wonder if she'd be willing to work at Nottingham, LLC?" He rubbed his left arm with his right hand. "I have no idea how the business is doing. I left David in charge and left."

Robert touched his left arm with his right hand. "Jonathan told me that David has tripled the business since you left. He said it's thriving."

"Uhm! I think it's time to revamp my thinking. Perhaps, David will stay in his position under me. This way, I can seek the Lord what he wants me to do. I love painting, but I'd really like to teach Bible." He bit his top lip. "Instead of being so involved in the business, I can let others who are gifted by the Lord to do it." He rubbed his left arm with his right hand. "I think my fear of losing the business had me leaning on my own understanding. I didn't support myself on faith in God and his word. Then after the accident, I blamed myself." He shook his head. "I don't know how I became so full of unbelief. It's like I said earlier, I allowed the weights of the business to be a burden to my faith. Then after the accident, I allowed the weight of grief to be a further burden. I became a man trying to control my situation without faith in God, until I was imprisoned in my grief and guilt. Thank God, he didn't leave me nor forsake me."

"God is so good."

"Amen! I truly do sense a new light in me. I'll always miss them, but an incredible healing took place Thursday night. I know it wasn't my fault." He rubbed his left arm with his right hand. "I did allow fear to overtake me instead of faith. Then when the accident happened, I allowed grief to consume me." He hung his head. "I do remember in the beginning hearing to walk in the spirit and ye shall not fulfill the lusts of the flesh. Instead of listening, I walked in the flesh. Grief is normal. But not when it consumes you, it becomes the god you serve."

"We know that all things work together for good to them that love God, to them who are the called according to his purpose. I believe God is going to use this experience of yours to not only bless you, but others. Many are going through grief and need to see if they take their eyes off the Lord and focus on the grief, they'll sink into despair."

"Yes, the Lord showed that with Peter walking on the water. As long as he kept his eyes on the Lord, he was fine. However, once he looked at the storm, he was about to sink." He blew out a heavy sigh. "I do wish I'd called out to the Lord for help like Peter did. Instead,

I allowed my flesh to believe I was responsible for their death." He threw up his hands. "Like I said yesterday, as if I'm the giver and taker of life. I knew when God ordains our time of death, nothing will stop it." He paused. "I don't know why it was their time, but God knows what he's doing." He turned to look at Robert. "I was so backwards that I even questioned God's love for me. I don't know how many times I've rebuked Christians who doubted God loved them."

"Sometimes, we have to walk in other people's shoes to understand where they're coming from." He touched Tom's right arm with his left hand. "I don't mean we let them think God doesn't love them, but God doesn't want us going around with a self-righteous attitude. We can all sin, and we have to remember it's only the grace of God that keeps us."

"I know now I felt contempt for anyone who didn't live the word. I really was self-righteous. God had to get me to this place in order for me to learn I must allow the Holy Spirit to lead me in my dealings with other Christians and not my stinking flesh. Yes, they need to be told truth, but not from someone who thought he was above sinning."

"Amen!" Robert said with tears streaming down his face. "I must admit God has put such a love in my heart for you. I feel like Paul who called Timothy his son. You are my son begotten in the Lord." He wiped his tears. "I don't know what God has planned, but you're definitely a part of the rest of my life."

"When you said that, I was shown Hannah and the twins." His eyebrows scrunched together. "Is God saying he wants them to be my family?" He paused. "Before I married Abigail, I felt the Lord wanted my children to be Mark and Faith. However, her parents were already dead, and she wanted them to be Samuel and Rachel. I struggled with it, for I knew the Lord told me my children were Mark and Faith. However, I relented." He laughed. "I do have to tell you when I read the story of what Hannah did in the Bible, I asked the Lord if I could marry a woman like Hannah." He felt his heart beat fast. "Please don't tell this to anyone. I don't want to be guilty of presumption."

Robert chuckled. "Let me tell you, son, if God is doing this, it will come to pass. He'll make things clear to all involved."

Jonathan, David, and Dr. Steinberg stood dumbfounded, mouths opened, and eyes bulging as Robert, Martha, Hannah, Mary, Jason, Leah, Helen, and the twins walked into church with Tom. Tom hurried over to Jonathan and hugged him. "It's so good to see you."

Jonathan's face beamed. "Praise the Lord!" He grabbed both of Tom's shoulders and stared into his face. "Tom, it's really you. You look wonderful." He paused. "You do look a little thin, but it's you."

David grabbed Tom and gave him a bear hug. "This is definitely a miracle." He stood back and gazed into Tom's eyes. "I saw what you looked like before you left." He paused. "Plus, I saw you through the window in the cottage." He grabbed Tom and gave him another bear hug. "This is a miracle."

Dr. Steinberg clasped his hands. "How did this happen?" He looked at Robert. "What did you do?"

"I kept seeking the Lord for a way to breach his cocoon of grief. Tom was so hidden inside that he seemed detached." He scratched the back of head with his left hand. "Anyway, as I was praying Faith interrupted me. When she did, I was quickened by the Lord on how to breach his cocoon. I was to say the names of Mark and Faith, and they were to introduce themselves to him." He gestured towards Tom with his left hand. "When I mentioned the names, he trembled. So, I said them again, and he really trembled. But when he looked up, his eyes looked into my face, and then he looked at Mark. By this time, his body was trembling so much that I knew something was happening."

Tom gestured with both hands. "By the time I got back to the cottage, I was in somewhat of a daze. Anyway, the Lord had me look at some pictures of my father. Although Robert resembles him, Mark could have been his twin." He paused. "While all this was happening, I heard something at my door. When I opened it, a toy poodle ran in. After that, the Lord did an incredible healing." He laughed. "I told the Lord I felt like King Nebuchadnezzar being healed. It's as if I came back from the dead and was completely restored."

Jonathan gestured with his hands. "I think we need to get into Sunday school. After church, we'll all get together at the Family Buffet and have a good time of fellowship."

Robert chuckled. "I agree. Besides, today is my first Sunday school class here."

Jonathan nodded. "Yes, lets' get there, and I'll get you introduced."

Once everyone was seated, Jonathan gestured towards Robert. "Class, this is Dr. Montgomery, our new adult Sunday school teacher. Dr. Montgomery taught at Fountain Bible College for years. I'm sure he's going to make Sunday school quite interesting for everyone." He paused. "Dr. Montgomery will also be our new counselor a few times a week to help Dr. Steinberg."

Tom whispered to Hannah. "I didn't know he was a doctor."

Hannah's blue eyes sparkled as she whispered. "He has a PhD in theology."

Robert got their attention. "Okay, let's pray before we start." He paused. "Thomas Nottingham, would you pray for our class?"

Tom's voice shook. "Lord, I can't thank you enough for this Sunday school class. I ask you to bless Dr. Montgomery, bless each in this class, and may we all come away wiser and more knowledgeable in your word. In Jesus Name, Amen!"

Everyone responded. "Amen!"

After the class, they all headed to the sanctuary. Jonathan rubbed his bald head with his right hand. "Well, Dr. Montgomery, I do believe you're an incredible teacher. The way you unfold the word. I was blessed sitting under you this morning." He bit the hangnail on his right hand. "Did you ever sense a call to the ministry?"

"The Lord told me he could have me pastor, but he had a greater need for me to teach. I felt him impress me with the sad truth that many are not being properly prepared in Bible College how to feed the sheep. Now, we have all kinds of churches with famines of the word. There's too much joking, worldly news, prosperity without self-denial, and worship that resembles a night club with dimmed lights, people dancing choreographed around the altar, etc. It's definitely not Holy Spirit led. It's all flesh appealing."

Jonathan gazed into Robert's eyes. "I know."

Martha touched her husband's right arm. "I do believe this will help me to run. I mean, I feel like I grew this morning." She paused. "Maybe not meat yet. I mean, I believe it was milk mixed with cereal."

Robert chuckled. "I love you! I'm glad you enjoyed it."

Jonathan had called the Family Buffet to say he'd need a larger table. When they arrived, Mr. Smith whispered to Jonathan. "Pastor Kregel, I prepared the small dining room for you and your party. It's usually booked on Sunday's, but it wasn't today." He laughed. "If you believe you'll need it every week, I'll book it permanently for you."

"I do believe I will. It seems like our little Sunday lunch group is no longer little."

Mr. Smith nodded. "Okay, if you'll all follow me, I'll show you to the dining room."

As they were heading toward the room, Mark and Faith both let go of Mary's hands and each took one of Tom's hands. Faith's little nose scrunched up. "Would you be my daddy? All the kids in my Sunday school class have daddy's."

Mark squeezed Tom's hand. "Grandfather can't be our daddy. You're the only one who can." He did a slight jump. "Please, please, be our daddy."

Faith started to jump up and down. "Yes, all the kids have to bring their daddy's to class next week for Father's Day. Can we bring you?"

Hannah's face was bright red. "Mark and Faith, you don't choose who your daddy is. Jesus must do that."

Faith's chin stuck out. "Jesus already did."

"What are you talking about?"

Mark nodded his head. "We prayed and asked Jesus who our daddy was, and he said it was Tom Nottingham."

Hannah's voice trembled. "Tom, I'm so sorry. I don't know what to say."

Tom laughed. "Out of the mouth of babes." He gazed into Hannah's eyes. "I can stand in as their daddy next week. It must be difficult for children not to have a daddy." He paused. "What I'm saying is I'll be honored to be their surrogate daddy next week."

Mark and Faith both jumped up and down and then hugged Tom. "We have a surrogate daddy!" They both said in unison.

Faith's little nose scrunched up. "What's a surrogate daddy?"

"It means I'll stand in as your daddy next Sunday. A real daddy would be someone who is your mommy's husband."

Hannah's voice trembled. "Are you sure this is the right thing to do? They're so impressionable."

Tom nodded. "I feel strongly to do it."

As they entered the dining room, Mary took the children's hands to seat them next to her. Robert took control of where everyone would sit. He sat Tom and Hannah next to each other, Martha next to him, Tabitha, Amos, and Joel next to Jonathan, David next to his wife Marilyn, Dr. Steinberg and his wife Jessica, Jason and Leah, and Helen. "Well, that takes care of the seating." He chuckled. "Now, let's get our meal." He paused. "Mary, I'll sit with the twins until you get their food. By that time, Hannah and Tom should be back with theirs, and you and I can get ours."

At first there was the usual bragging about the food, and a little small talk. Robert felt his stomach flutter as he stood up to get everyone's attention. "Excuse me for interrupting your meal, but I believe the Lord wants the light to shine as the noonday sun here today."

As Tom heard Robert, he felt his heart beat against his chest. "I'm about to step out on the water, but the impression is so strong in me. I'm not sure if you all can hear my heart beating against my chest."

Hannah clasped both hands against her heart. "I believe I'm to step out on the water with you."

Tom went down on one knee and took her right hand in both of his. "Hannah Montgomery will you do me the honor of becoming my wife?"

Hannah took a napkin with her left hand and fanned herself. "I dreamed this last night." She cleared her throat. "When I woke up, I immediately went into prayer for such nonsense. I'd only known you a couple of weeks, and we never even spoke until yesterday." She giggled. "What I'm trying to say is this is God. I won't kick against the pricks." She looked into Tom's eyes. "I will."

The whole table was in rejoicing and praising the Lord. Jonathan ran over and hugged Tom. "I knew God had something special planned for Hannah and the twins. I thought it was Dr. Montgomery adopting her." He grabbed his head with both hands. "I'm overwhelmed by all this. God is awesome!"

Robert and Martha both hugged Tom and Hannah. Robert had tears streaming down his cheeks. "Tom, you'll actually be my son now."

Everyone was giving their congratulations when Faith's nose scrunched up. "I don't see Tom and Mommy stepping on water."

Mark showed the palms of his hands and shrugged his shoulders. "Why is everyone happy about them stepping on water. Are we going to the lake?"

Tom laughed and picked up Faith. "It means I'm going to be your real daddy, not one who stands in for your Sunday school class."

www.ingramcontent.com/pod-product-compliance
Lightning Source LLC
Chambersburg PA
CBHW071314200626
46813CB00015B/2198